MADNESS IN MANHATTAN MINE

Kyle J. Durrant

*This is for
Shannon,
My guiding moonlight*

VELOX BOOKS
Published by arrangement with the author.

Madness in Manhattan Mine copyright © 2023 by Kyle J. Durrant.

All Rights Reserved.

This book is a work of fiction. People, places, events, and situations are the product of the author's imagination. Any resemblance to actual persons, living or dead, or historical events, is purely coincidental.

No part of this book may be reproduced, stored in a retrieval system, or transmitted by any means without the written permission of the author and publisher.

CHAPTER 1
WELCOME TO MANHATTAN

As I write this record, the dust and detritus that once was the town of Manhattan drifts down from the heavens, like grey snow whose flakes are made not of icy crystals but the smoldering cells of some hundred lost souls. That I am the only one to escape is an injustice of divine extent. Perhaps this is my purgatory: to walk free of the crater, carrying the weight of their demise on my shoulders.

Forgive me, I should explain.

No doubt you see the crater and have walked or driven through the ashes of Manhattan that surely still fall; I am certain you heard the explosion, which I would not be surprised to learn was heard in every neighboring state. Perhaps you even saw the greenish-grey cloud that rocketed into the heavens, or felt the shockwave that rendered my vehicle immobile.

It falls upon me, now, as the sole survivor, to explain the circumstances that have culminated in this disaster.

The date was May 27th. It was a hot, cloudless day, as are many days in the desert, and my trusty Ford Fiesta rumbled steadily along the not-roads that led to the small former mining town of Manhattan, Nevada. An oft-forgotten place, owing to its much better-known namesake, my knowledge of the town's existence was owed almost entirely to the presence of my uncle, who had been a resident there for the past fifty-seven years.

Before that it had been home to my father, and his father, and his father's father, but I had never heard mention of the place from anyone's lips. My father had left long before I was born, after all, and had always been reticent about discussing his childhood. That was until I completed my studies in history and sociology at Miskatonic University, at least.

There I had fallen in love with the dawn and death of the gold rush and the myriad mines that had fallen into disrepair since. Stories of lifeless towns inhabited only by dust and rusting minecarts awakened an unquenchable curiosity within me. No sooner had I graduated than I announced my intention to dig into and write about the history of abandoned mines across the nation.

It was a shock when my father made offhand mention of a heretofore unknown uncle. He had, my father told me, remained in what he called "a cursed town of misfortune and misery that molders and crumbles around an old, abandoned mine". I rejoiced to know that I possessed a personal—if suppressed—connection to my newfound obsession.

Therefore, it was with Manhattan that my mission began. Unfortunately, it is also with Manhattan that my mission has ended.

It truly was a desolate space, nestled discretely at the bottom of a rocky ridge, resembling a ghost town from one of those old Westerns they rerun every weekend at midnight. Run-down wooden buildings, rusty water tower, no asphalt on the roads, and the whistle of the wind. You could be forgiven for believing you had, indeed, stepped onto a movie set, except for the fact there were people who wandered wistfully along its sandy streets. When a tumbleweed rolled along the road in front of me, I was only shocked because until now I hadn't realized they were a real phenomenon.

I had expected my presence to be met by long, dirty glares, but it seemed I was the ghost here, drifting by like an invisible entity on the wind. The rumble of my Fiesta was noticed only once, when an elderly gentleman in faded denim dungarees was readying to cross the road with the carefree ease customary in a small town with little-to-no traffic. His widened eyes and panicky back-step drew forth a chuckle, but his fearful expression as he recovered prompted me to hide my smile and raise a hand in apology.

He huffed for a moment, but then eased and nodded back to me. Forgive and forget.

Having arrived at this forgotten and crumbling town, my attentions now turned to locating my uncle's home. He still lived, my father assured me, at the old family property on the edge of town. I had a crudely drawn map at the ready, and a vivid description of the house I was to find.

It did not prove as easy as I had hoped, however.

My father's map was even less clear than expected, making no use of landmarks—what few there were—or even street names. Admittedly, it had been many years since he had been to Manhattan, and he seemed loath to discuss the place with me, but when he had offered to draw up a map to help me reach my uncle, I had hoped he would have enough knowledge stored away to prove useful.

I would argue, then, that it was only by providence that I arrived at a house matching the description given by my father, though many of the houses along the way differed little. White paint peeling, revealing brown wood rotting to black, with clouded windows like brackish water; a round aperture blocked off by boards stood out from the roof, and the front door appeared five-times replaced, its paint fresher but colored entirely different from the rest of the house, its narrow window empty of glass but for perhaps a single shard stuck in its frame.

Approaching the building, bathed in the shadows of the cliff face that towered barely ten feet away, but dripping with perspiration regardless, I could not help but fear my uncle was either dead or had left long ago without telling my father, for how else could this house be in such an awful state.

One of the steps leading up to the door bent drastically under my weight, urging me to skip the next one to plant my feet safely at the doorstep. Wind-chimes sang from somewhere out of sight, though the air was deathly still. There was no hint of movement from within the house.

Steeling myself against a grisly discovery, I knocked on the door. Paint flaked off beneath my knuckles. The echo of the impact carried deep into the house. I breathed out slowly, waiting before I knocked again, more paint flaking.

Floorboards creaked behind the door, followed by the rattling of metal chains. The lock groaned, and then the door inched open, hinges protesting despite the minute movement. A sliver of light lanced inside, striking a pale face. Wincing, the figure inside scanned me with dark eyes.

'Hmm...' it grumbled. 'You look just like him; got the same judgy frown.'

I stammered upon hearing him, his voice the closest thing I could imagine to sandpaper if it could talk. 'Uncle Albert?' I asked.

'Just Bert will do fine,' he replied, fiddling with a chain on the other side of the door. It jingled as it fell free, and he opened the door further, the hinges screaming. 'So, you're Maxwell?' He looked me up and down, lingering on my glasses, then on a tattoo with no real meaning that peeked out from my sweaty t-shirt. 'Yep... just like your father, I'll say. Bit more nervous, perhaps, but just like him otherwise. Come on, come on, in you come.'

He turned and limped his way back into the house, leaving me to close the door behind us. The whine was unbearable in the confines of the lobby, so I was thankful once the door was closed and once again silent. 'Max,' I said, hoping he could still hear me. 'I prefer Max.'

'Well, Max,' he replied, 'come and sit down. Don't worry about the lock just yet.'

I don't think I'd ever been in a house quite so forlorn. Footprints left in a layer of dust led me through to an even dustier lounge, sparsely furnished. A handful of faded pictures hung on the walls, ghostly faces watching me as I shuffled around a lopsided table topped with coverless books. As I sat down upon a worn armchair, a dusty cloud like smoke erupted to consume me. Coughing and wafting my hands, it eventually cleared; my uncle stared at me, meeting my eyes.

'Yeah, I know. It's a state. What do you expect, Max? You saw the condition of the town on your way here; there's not a single house in Manhattan that's much better than this.' He leant back in his torn, tatty armchair and sighed. 'Like I said: you've got the same judgy frown.'

'It's nothing against you,' I replied, fearful of offending a relative I had only just been acquainted with. 'I've just never…'

'No, no, it's fine, Max. Your father got out of here for a reason; if he hadn't taken most of our old pa's money to do it, I wouldn't be here either.' He sighed and patted at his shirt pocket. 'Curse it, I'm out of cigarettes!'

Ignoring his comment about my father and, being a non-smoker, unable to help him with his predicament, I instead sought to distract him with my reason for being there. 'I suppose it's safe to assume there's not much money or work around here nowadays.' He stopped searching himself for cigarettes and looked back at me. 'It was a mining town years ago, right?' He nodded, still silent. 'And without the mine, there's not much reason for people being here. So…' His lips cracked into a thin smile. '… why are there still people here?'

Uncle Bert shuffled in his seat, straightening out, eyes still on mine. 'Plenty of people left when the mine closed. Plenty of people were stuck here; some had put everything they owned into this town. Others, like your great grandpa, just couldn't bring themselves to leave. He used to say that Manhattan had sunk its claws into some of the folk who moved here. Some of the miners. My old pa used to say he'd see your great grandpa wander up to the mine even after it closed, helmet on, and just stand at the entrance for an hour before wandering home looking like death himself.

'A handful of shops managed to stay open, and we got supplies coming in frequent enough to keep people alive. Police force dwindled down from three men to one; we got a two-man town council 'round here that keeps people happy enough. But no one's got the money to leave. Hell, most outsiders don't know the place even exists, and that's including government types I'll bet. We might as well not exist, but we make do…'

He sighed, eyes heavy.

'Same thing happened all over the country,' I muttered, more to myself than my uncle, but I saw him nod. 'But… I couldn't say there are any other towns that have survived. Not unless they've been forgotten like this one.' He chuckled. 'Usually, the families just dwindle and die; there's no new blood, so no one marries, no one has kids.'

Bert peered toward his filthy windows, as if he could actually see something through them. 'Well, you didn't hear it from me, but some folks around here don't much care about "new blood".' He cackled. 'But you're right, the town is dying. Those who can leave are gone, and soon it'll just be the old and the inbred left behind.' He cackled again. 'But that's just what happens, Max. Mines go dry, the companies that dug 'em up move on, and the people are left to do what they can.'

Now it was my turn to nod along, his words sinking in. My research, though, had to go deeper than the nihilistic mutterings of my decrepit uncle. I needed to know exactly when the mine closed down, how many people left, and what exactly had happened in the time since to those who had stayed behind.

'Does the town have a records office?' I asked.

'The town hall has some records,' he replied, shrugging. 'Never been much need for a proper records office; hell, the town hall isn't exactly a hall, either. Barely bigger than this place.' He gestured around the room. 'Not sure you'll find much there, but I won't stop you. Don't want you to think I'm trying to kick you out of town or nothing.' Another cackle, this time sending shivers up my spine. 'There's no hotel or anything, just so you know, so you're welcome to stay here. I'll clean up a bit, seeing as I'll be having company.'

I smiled at him, albeit weakly. 'Thank you, Uncle Bert. I'll... I'll probably have a quick look around town, and maybe at the town hall, but I'll be back by evening.' I clambered out of my chair; Bert remained seated, nodding, and waved his hand toward the door.

'Alright then. I'd tell you to be careful, but the only thing you've got to be scared of is the sand.'

I found myself smiling at the thought, but then he made a remark that, despite its triviality, and for reasons beyond my comprehension, swept it away and wrapped my chest in icy chains:

'Even the coyotes seem to have forgotten this place exists.'

CHAPTER 2
THE SECRETS OF MANHATTAN MINE

Sand sprayed my face as I wandered the streets of Manhattan, carried on a dry desert wind. It was approaching midday, the sun high overhead, and my shirt clung to my body. Glad as I was that I hadn't chosen to wear a full, button-down shirt, I still found my clothes stifling and ducked into shade whenever possible.

This was not often.

On one occasion, I entered one of Manhattan's few shops, a convenience store with very few conveniences, where I was able to purchase some bottled water and an expired sandwich. The clerk, a middle-aged woman with greying-brown hair, studied me carefully as I brought my items to the counter. "You're not from around here, are you?" she asked.

'No,' I replied, setting my purchase down, struck by the clichéd nature of her words. 'I'm Albert Wolfe's nephew; I'm staying with him whilst I do some research.'

'Research?' she inquired; she was yet to touch the water or sandwich. 'There's not much to research around here, unless you're interested in dying towns.'

My smile seemed unwelcome, but it emerged, nonetheless. 'Truthfully, that's kind of why I'm here. I'm looking into abandoned mines across America, and trying to discover their stories, and the stories of the towns that grew around them. I didn't even know this place existed until I found out about my uncle.'

'Yes, well,' she began, punching in the price for my meal, 'there's not much to be said about Manhattan. Mine opened, went dry, got closed down, and some people were stupid enough to stick around. Four dollars.'

Handing over the money, I said, 'My uncle told me some people felt like they couldn't leave.'

'No money, like my grandma,' she replied with a shrug. 'You have a good day, young man.'

Nodding, I took my lunch and left, grateful if a little disappointed with what she'd had to say about the town.

From there, I carried on along the sandy streets, using what few signs existed to lead me toward the town hall. I encountered no one else along the way, for they were no doubt sensible enough to avoid the heat, and eventually came upon the building I was looking for.

At a glance, I would have missed it, had it not been for the sizeable, if shoddy, sign planted in the grassless ground in front of it.

It read, "TO N HAL".

The building itself was in just as sorry a state, with missing shutters and windows, both broken and boarded. It had once been painted red, I could tell, though scraps of faded color remained only in sparse patches around windows and along panels obscured by straggly shrubs. Every room appeared bathed in shadow, though I could imagine this was as a result of the day's natural light drowning out whatever artificial sources may operate within.

As I made my way inside, I recalled the decrepitude of Uncle Bert's property and half-expected the distressed door to fall free of its hinges. I was, thankfully, wrong. The lobby was an empty affair, with only a single seat and a desk, neither of which were anywhere close to one another. Upon the desk sat a small bell, which I rang. Hovering by the desk, I was waiting long enough that I was about to ring the bell again when a stick-like woman with ash grey hair and skin equally ashen emerged from a nearby room and stepped up in front of me.

'Not often we get visitors,' she remarked.

'The lady at the store said something similar,' I joked; she didn't smile. Clearing my throat, I continued, 'I'm Max Wolfe—Albert Wolfe's nephew. I was hoping to have a look at the town records.' She cocked an eyebrow. 'I'm hoping to write a book about the hows and whys of abandoned mines.'

She analyzed me, much as my uncle had, unblinking eyes roving over my face. 'There's not much to say about Manhattan Mine,' she said at last. 'Just as they all do eventually, it ran dry. Most people left with the company; a few foolish families stuck around. If you're that interested, though, there's some stuff in the cellar. Mainly just employment records—what little they actually bothered with back then—and a few bits of documentation the company left behind.' Finally, a smile, though it was twisted and obviously forced. 'It'll all tell the same story, Mr Wolfe: the mine failed, and Manhattan was forgotten.'

'Whatever information I can get to aid in my research will be much appreciated,' I said.

The lady nodded. 'Well, I suppose you should come with me so I can open up the room for you.'

She led me further into the lobby, along the side of a staircase leading up to the second floor. A door was set into the side of it, which she unlocked with a small key. Swinging it open, a torrent of dust whirled out to meet us. The both of us coughed, and as it settled, she handed me the key.

'Stick it on the desk when you're done down there.'

'Thank you,' I said. 'I didn't catch your name.'

'You're not going to be here long enough to need it,' she replied sharply, disappearing back into the room from which she had emerged.

I located a cord just inside the cellar entrance; the sickly light that flickered to life offered little illumination, but it was enough for me to find my way down the narrow, rickety staircase and into the cellar. At first, I was astounded that the room could be so cold, considering the sweltering heat outside; goosebumps prickled on my arms, eliciting a shiver. It did not take long for me to put such thoughts to the back of my mind, overcoming the change of temperature and focusing on the matter at hand.

Stone-walled and sandy-floored, it was clear to me that the preservation of documentation was not a priority for the administration of Manhattan. From what the lady of ash had told me I could imagine that much had already been lost, and little in the way of accurate record-keeping had occurred since the mine's closing.

Leaning wooden shelves lined the cold walls, inches from collapse, sparsely laden with torn boxes and scattered stacks of paper. Nothing was clearly labelled; indeed, most of what I saw was frustratingly unmarked by categorization or identification. My hopes of entering the cellar and simply picking up such records as pertained to my research were quashed, leaving me instead in the unenviable position of perusing every crumbling box and faded document to find what material was relevant.

It struck me that there could not be a single person of a scholarly mindset in this entire town. They, like me, would have thought it unthinkable to leave these documents in such disarray.

There was, fortunately, a table at the center of the room, with a pair of chairs around it that, upon inspection, proved sturdy enough for use. Though caked in dust, I found there were yet more papers upon the table—unfortunately, these papers proved to be faded, smudged or otherwise despoiled. My first act once I had familiarized myself with these squalid surroundings was to wipe off as much dust as I dared without choking upon the dry cloud. Then I turned to the unsteady shelves and, with great care so as not to displace the fragile equilibrium holding them intact, retrieved the first of many boxes.

Digging through its contents, I found little in relation to the mine itself, but a bounty of information regarding the shopfronts and saloons that had come and gone throughout Manhattan's century or so of existence.

Many had, it seemed, survived for years with almost constant ownership by one person or another. Others had been owned by one of two people with the name of "Bergmann". These records suggested an uninterrupted period of prosperity until, within the space of a single twelve-month period, almost every commercial property in the town closed its doors forever. That year was 1909. Along with this document was a sudden absence of references to any enterprises owned by the Bergmanns.

What records I read suggested that those who remained had managed to stay in business ever since, and supposedly there were six such shops still operating in Manhattan. Having located one so far, I resolved to write down the other five and seek them out. Whatever questions remained once I had completed my reading of the records here could possibly be answered by the town's few business owners.

I did not return the box to its place on the shelf, fearing it would cause a collapse and then, in turn, a domino effect of tumbling shelves. Instead, I simply replaced the documents and left the box upon the table.

The next box I removed from the shelves, just as carefully as I had the first, contained what appeared to be census forms from a myriad of different years. I removed one document with excess enthusiasm, and its edges crumbled in my grip. After that, I made certain to treat the rest with the respect they deserved. They showed a drastic decrease in the population of Manhattan in the years 1908 and 1909. Skimming through the lists I found the name of my great-grandpa, Otto Gustav Wolfe, who, like many other townsfolk of that year, was listed in the 1909 list as a "former employee of the Bergmann Brothers Mining Company".

Though I still sought to uncover more information, what little I had found already confirmed in my mind that the mine had closed sometime in 1908. That it was owned by the Bergmanns was, in itself, a major find, for it certainly suggested that the prosperity of Manhattan was directly tied to their success.

Discovering the year of closure was valuable information; it revealed that this small, dying town had somehow struggled on without any real means of income for more than a century. Others, I was sure, would have died out long ago, but somehow Manhattan had survived.

Was it due to the mysterious desire to remain that had so enraptured people such as my great grandpa? Had it not been for this strange phenomenon, would the town have emptied all the quicker, leaving just a desolate assembly of empty buildings?

Further analysis of the poorly kept documents gave me only tiny tidbits of information, most of which simply supported my conclusion that the mine had closed in 1908, and the Bergmann Brothers had left alongside so many others. Unfortunately, much of what I found appeared particularly incomplete; there were years of missing employment records, and when I gave the census lists a second skim, I realized that some names had actually been expunged, whereas I had originally assumed the documents were simply damaged.

Amongst leftover records from the mining company itself I found numerous allusions to the discovery of multiple glory-holes full of gold, silver and various other precious minerals. All of these discoveries took place between 1900 and 1907. Soon enough, I was digging out every document I could find, and cross-referencing them I started to realize that the town's accumulated wealth had actually been steadily increasing up until the year of 1908. Moreover, one of the last recorded surveys I could find, also dated 1908, had uncovered what the scratched, crumpled, and most illegible record called a "motherlode".

Admittedly, there were a great many missing pieces of the puzzle, but I found little to suggest any signs of the mine running dry in the lead-up to its sudden closure in 1908. If anything, it appeared that the Bergmann Brothers had owned one of the most profitable mines in all of America.

The closer to 1908 the records got, however, the fewer and more far between the entries became. There were some mentions of gas pockets, and of a handful of casualties, but these were normal things in mines, especially in the days where worker safety was of less than paramount concern. What all of these meagre mentions agreed upon, however, was that the mine was producing considerable yield.

I leant back in my seat, unaware of how long I had been there, but nursing a headache nonetheless. Pinching the bridge of my nose I attempted to process the cavalcade of information I had hammered into my head, but the ache in my skull and the itching of my eyes proved too distracting. Only one conclusion was clear in my mind: the mine had closed in 1908, but the true reasoning for its closure was something altogether different from the explanation I had heard around town.

Had an incident of some kind had happened in the Manhattan Mine? Something the Bergmann Brothers and, by extension, the community of Manhattan had deigned significant enough to cause the closure of their mine?

My thoughts returned to the missing employment records and altered census data; to the bounty of wealth that had been extracted from the mine; to the recent discovery of a "motherlode"; to the sudden exodus of almost all of Manhattan's populace.

Something was wrong about all this, I realized, and it was in that moment I decided I had to uncover the strange secret of the Manhattan Mine.

If I'd only known what chilling discoveries awaited me, perhaps I would have bid my uncle goodbye and left that town forever.

CHAPTER 3
REVELATIONS AND MYSTERIES

It was growing dark by the time I returned to my uncle's house, the sweltering heat replaced by an inescapable chill. The sky overhead was completely clear of clouds, bathed in faded purple light as the sun disappeared over the desert horizon. The stars sparkled overhead, brighter than I'd ever seen them.

Never had I been able to take the time to appreciate the beauty of the cosmos, which is so often obscured by the light of cities. Despite the biting cold of the night desert air, I stopped beyond the threshold of the house to gaze heavenward and watch the little lights dance in the purple-hued blackness.

The night sky is a deceptively simple thing; what we see is but a fraction of what exists beyond the veils of time and distance. How many of the stars we see are even still burning? What unthinkable distances separate the stars we think of as Orion's Belt? So many mysteries beneath the surface.

Much like Manhattan, I considered.

With the night air wrapping about me like a frigid blanket, I dragged my eyes away from the darkness above and entered my uncle's house. The door remained unlocked, and I wondered whether that was out of good manners or neglect.

Courtesy, it seemed, was a concept known to my uncle. As promised, the old man had taken it upon himself to clean up the house; dust still caked the floor and many surfaces, but he had tidied the stack of books upon the table, brushed down the chairs, and swept previously unnoticed dirt and debris into a neat pile in a corner of the room.

Having not seen any of the house beyond the lounge, I could only assume he had done similar work elsewhere. As long as there was a bed available for me that wouldn't have me bitten across every inch of my being, I was happy.

Despite the late hour, I found my uncle awake, sat in the kitchen which lay just beyond the lounge. He cocked his head at me as I approached, but smiled as I entered the light of the kitchen.

A dirty plate sat on the table in front of him. Dusty cupboards and dilapidated countertops formed a barely functional kitchen, but his stove appeared in working order, and there was enough unbroken space available for the preparation of a simple meal.

I saw no sink but assumed Uncle Bert had some means of cleaning his crockery.

'Wasn't sure when to expect you,' he said, inviting me to sit at the table. The chair creaked under my weight, though it was stronger than expected. 'You've been out long enough to explore the whole town. Not very impressive, hm?'

'Honestly, I haven't seen much of the town just yet,' I replied, rubbing at my eyes. 'I've been digging through the records.'

His face dropped; the smile vanished. 'Oh. Straight to business, is it?' He shook his head. 'Lord, you're just like your father. So impatient.'

'I fully intend to properly explore the town tomorrow,' I retorted. 'But yes, my priority is research. I'm sorry if that rubs you the wrong way.'

He scoffed, folding his arms. 'Yes, yes, and how's that working out for you? What startling revelations have you uncovered about this dried-up little backwater?'

My frown came unbidden, tempered by a heat in my chest and a flushing of my cheeks. In that instant, I could not tell if I was angry or embarrassed; probably both. Either way, my uncle took notice of my response and smiled at me.

'Out with it, then. I'm no mind-reader, Max my boy, but I can see you actually mean to tell me something.'

Though the warmth in my face lingered, the muscles of my brow relaxed, my demeanor softening. 'Do you make a habit of riling up family?' I grumbled, though the corners of my mouth twitched.

'I make a habit of riling up everyone,' he chuckled, patting me on the shoulder. 'Go on, then. Tell me what you found, and I'll let you know whether it's anything to get worked up about.'

Fighting the urge to roll my eyes, I adjusted my position in the chair so I could properly face Uncle Bert. 'Tell me again why the mine closed down.'

'It ran dry,' he replied with a shrug. 'It's what mines do. It ran dry, the company left, and poor schmucks like my grandpa got stuck here, either by choice or because they couldn't do anything else.'

'Were you aware, then,' I asked, 'that before the mine closed down, they found numerous gloryholes? Gold, silver, even diamonds.' His eyes widened, and I could feel a smirk fighting to form upon my face. 'They were still uncovering more deposits right up until 1908.'

'That's when the mine closed,' Bert breathed, slack-jawed and flopping back into his chair. 'I don't understand. They'd hit the jackpot; why did they abandon it?'

'I don't know,' I replied—it was the most honest statement I've ever made. My next was the most foolish. 'But I'm going to find out.'

***

The following day, after a restless night on an old mattress with stabbing springs—I had had to lay atop my pillows, which smelt stale and moldy, in order to accomplish any degree of comfort—my uncle offered to walk with me up to the mine itself. From there, he told me, I would be able to see most of the town, and he could point out particular places of interest for my research.

That the news of unexcavated gold and silver had excited him could not be denied, and he was quick to warn me not to make mention of it to anyone else in the town. I was grateful for his newfound eagerness, but frightfully aware his interest was not in the history—and mystery—of the mine, but in the wealth within.

Climbing up the rocky road proved a difficult undertaking for the both of us, due in no small part to the steep incline and the persistent pounding of the sun's blinding presence. I had suggested driving, but my uncle laughed at the idea. As we navigated the sharp, sizeable boulders that littered the route, I was inclined to agree with his judgement.

We spoke very little, focusing more on our breathing than conversation. Halfway up the forgotten road, we paused to lean against the remains of a rockslide and catch our breath. Standing there we could see the desert as it stretched out for miles, with Manhattan town in front of us; the horizon simply faded away into nothing. There wasn't another settlement in sight, and I even took the time to watch the sky for planes.

There was nothing.

'You can understand how this place gets forgotten,' my uncle said, smiling to himself. 'Middle of nowhere. A little town built at the bottom of a cliff. No one would see Manhattan; just the ridge of rock we're standing on now.'

Manhattan didn't look small from our vantage point—my great-grandpa had, after all, walked up this same road almost nightly after the mine was closed, or so my uncle said—but there remained a strange divide between the mine and the town. To me they felt like two separate places, as though the mine had existed long before the town, and it was only by happenstance that this was where people had decided to settle.

I looked down upon the myriad buildings, all built on the same basic template and set apart only by the occasional spire or extra window in the roof. The town hall was almost invisible amongst the architecture, but I found it. The town's church, I realized, was at the farthest point from the mine, which explained why I had not yet passed it.

We did not linger there long, however, and were soon continuing the modest trek to the mine.

'I'm beginning to wonder,' my uncle panted as we approached the top of the ridge, 'whether my grandpa walked all the way up here because he knew about the gold.' He held onto my arm for support, his limp particularly noticeable now. 'That would make sense, don't you think? He stuck around because he knew there was still gold in there; he came up here to dig, maybe, in the hopes of getting rich.' A wheezy laugh broke from his throat. 'I was about to wonder why he never told my pa, or us, but he probably didn't trust us to keep our mouths shut.'

Half-carrying Bert over the last crest of the road, I laughed with him, though I wasn't sure whether I was genuinely amused or simply too exhausted to formulate a proper response.

The mine entrance, little more than rotten wood around a hole going down into the ground at a forty-five-degree angle, was surrounded by rocks, rusted carts and collapsed shacks. Bert took a seat on a rock about the size of his armchair and wiped sweat from his brow, whilst I, no less sweaty, milled around the entrance and gazed down into the inky, musty blackness.

Stale air rose from the pit; I didn't linger near it for long.

Instead, I paced toward the edge of the ridge, where the town stretched out below me. The buildings were still big, appearing somewhere between an expensive though neglected dollhouse and the real thing, but the illusion of distance was enough to turn the town into a neglected diorama in someone's dusty loft.

'How many of those houses do you think are empty?' my uncle asked from behind me.

'Most of them,' I replied with a shrug. 'How many people still live here?'

'Believe it or not, there's somewhere around a hundred people still clinging on in Manhattan. You don't see anyone much, though; everyone squeezes into the church on Sunday, god-fearing or not, and half the town will lurk in Martha's bar most of the week, but beyond that most folk around here try to stay at home. The Barker boy comes to my place once a week to deliver some food.

'I think we're all just waiting to die. Manhattan is dying, and so are we, but none of us are so full of despair that we'll end things ourselves. So, we sit around, drinking, smoking, and waiting to fall asleep and not wake up. If they knew what we know, though, all that drinking and smoking would be replaced by digging, I think. The whole town would be climbing up this road every morning and digging to find what our grandpas couldn't.

'But that's our secret, right Max? Say, how about we dig it out ourselves? Then you won't have to worry about your book; won't have to dig around looking for answers to mysteries that no longer matter. You start asking questions, people might start wondering for themselves what's hidden in there, and then what? Madness in Manhattan, Max. That's what. Madness in Manhattan.'

Throughout my uncle's rambling rant of a reply, I continued gazing down at the town below. The people of Manhattan went about their dreary lives as little more than shuffling shadows. True enough, many of the individuals I saw had a common destination in mind, disappearing into a building that was one-part Old West saloon, one-part dive bar. A large sign hung above its door, but the paint was worn away enough that whatever words were upon it were illegible from so far away.

'Aren't you curious why the mine was closed?' I asked my uncle once he fell silent, facing him. A tiny whirlwind of sand spiraled at the dark maw of the mine. 'All that wealth yet to be dug up, and the Bergmann Brothers suddenly close it down, seal it up and leave; doesn't that strike you as odd?'

'Well, yes,' he replied. 'But I don't want to go drawing attention to it; if I can get even a little bit of that money, I can get out of this miserable hellhole.'

I shook my head. Whilst I understood his plight and the rush of hope he was no doubt experiencing, my academic mind could not stand by whilst this mystery went unsolved. 'Something about this just isn't right. I told you last night, uncle: I'm going to find out what happened.'

He sighed. 'Well, if you're that intent on finding out—and your old uncle's desperation won't sway you—then you've got a couple of options that I can think of.' He rose from the rock and came to stand beside me, turning me so we were looking out over the town—I admit, for half a second I thought he had intended to throw me off the ridge. 'You've exhausted your research in the records office, right?' I nodded. The records were either incomplete, missing or expunged. 'Then you could try asking around at Martha's place' He pointed at the old saloon. 'There are those other shops I mentioned, but they won't know nothing; probably won't care to talk to you either except to demand money. Maybe you could try the church, but they'll just lecture you about the greed of the miners causing the downfall of Manhattan, which isn't much help to you.

'Your other option is to dig in there.' He pointed over his shoulder. 'I don't know how much of the mine they sealed off, or how sturdy the props are, but there's nothing like a bit of hands-on investigation.' He jabbed my ribs with his elbow.

I peered back over our shoulders, towards the inky entrance to the forsaken, mysterious mine. It stared right back at me, daring me to do as my uncle suggested. The wooden beams tempted me with the false comfort of stability and safety, despite the darkness that seethed around them.

'Maybe once I've got some more information,' I said, only half-aware of my words. 'I'll get some equipment after I've spoken with some people.'

Uncle Bert clapped me on the back, shaking me out of the unusual trance that had captured me. 'I've still got some of grandpa's gear at the house. You go and do your weird university research stuff, and I'll dig the gear out for you. Let me know what you find out over dinner.'

He shuffled away, heading back down the steep, stony slope.

Alone atop the ridge, I looked out across the town of Manhattan again. Someone amongst the hundred or so inhabitants had to have the answers I sought, I was certain. Why else would they still be here? I decided in that moment that nothing was going to stop me from finding them.

CHAPTER 4
LIES, DAMNED LIES, AND COVER-UPS

I was not surprised to find all eyes on me as I entered Martha's place, notebook in hand. It was like a scene from a western, as the outsider steps into the criminal cowboys' territory. Unlike those films, however, I was not immediately confronted by an angry man with an oiled moustache. Instead, I heard only the furtive whispers of a few townsfolk, and felt the piercing eyes of the broad-shouldered, middle-aged woman at the bar.

Clearing my throat, I walked hesitantly towards her, dust drifting around me. It seemed everywhere I went in this town I found dust, so thick it was like entering an ancient ruin left to the mercies of time.

The streets on the way had been empty. No cars, aside from one rusted wreck parked up outside a boarded-up launderette, and few people. Many of those I passed seemed headed in the same direction as me, though moved at a straggler's pace, hands buried deep in their pockets and eyes gazing at the footsteps of ghosts.

Clearly, they knew the route by heart, carried almost entirely by muscle memory. Their lazy, trudging steps kicked up sand that billowed across the desolate roads in weak whirlwinds, and I found myself coughing every time I passed them by.

Soon enough, however, I had found myself at Martha's, her name written in faded, blocky lettering above the door. I'd struggled to make out the detail from the ridge, and even from directly in front of it I could barely identify the letters. At a glance, it seemed the sign had once been marked by more words, but whatever had been there had faded away long ago.

Taking a seat at the bar, I was handed a half glass of whiskey before a single word could work itself free of my lips.

'What dragged you into this godforsaken place?' she asked without meeting my eyes. Leaning against the bar, staring out into the dusty space, it seemed as though she were speaking to a ghost.

'I'm just doing some research,' I replied, swirling the amber liquid around the glass. No ice; of course there was no ice.

A laugh barked from her throat. 'Research? Here? I tell you, you're the first visitor this town has had in decades, and research is no reason to visit. How did you even know the place exists?'

This time it was my throat that formed the laugh. 'I thought news travelled fast in small towns.' She didn't seem to register my comment; not even a raised eyebrow. 'I'm Albert Wolfe's nephew. He's the only reason I know the place exists.'

'Oh, still alive, is he?' Finally, she turned to face me, her expression giving nothing away. There was a peculiar darkness in her eyes as she said, 'I thought the cigarettes killed him years ago. He doesn't come down here anymore, you see. Used to be a regular.'

'His health isn't so great,' I said with a shrug. Hardly a lie; with his limp and the cigarettes, it was more than believable. 'He was the one who pointed me this way, though. Said I could probably learn a few things about the town here.'

She shuffled along the bar to stand directly across from me. Her lips twisted into the slightest sneer. 'What exactly are you researching, hm? Looking into the incest rates in backwater towns? Studying the mortality rates of babies born without proper nutrition? There's nothing positive about this place, and your uncle should have told you as much.' She sighed, and the sneer subsided. 'Drink up, young man, and then be on your way, before the town sinks its claws into you too.'

Processing her words, I sipped from my drink. Upon the first taste I could tell it was heavily watered down, though knew I shouldn't be surprised. Where, indeed, was a struggling town such as this to source its alcohol from? There was certainly no brewery—the records had told me that much at least—and what supplies came to this place were likely paltry at best.

'I've got no intention of staying for long,' I explained after another short sip. 'As I said, I'm just here to do my research and then be on my way. As for what I'm researching...' My shoulder twitched and I quickly surveyed the bar. There weren't as many eyes on me now—most of the patrons were now returning their attentions to their drinks—but some still lingered. More bodies had shambled in whilst I spoke. Let them hear, I decided. They'd either avoid me or offer me some answers.

Turning my attention back to Martha, I found she had turned her back on me and was grabbing herself a bottle of beer from a lifeless refrigerator. Raising my voice by the mildest margin, I continued, 'I'm just interested in the history of abandoned mines across the country. How some led to the emptying of their towns, whilst others somehow thrived after the mines were closed, and all of the examples in-between. Like Manhattan.'

Martha deftly uncapped her beer against the wood of the bar, marked with several hundred scratchings from similar actions. 'Have you been to the town hall? They've got some stuff in the basement.'

I nodded. 'Yes, I have. Thank you. I found… a few things to get me started.' How much should I say? I asked myself. Uncle Bert had extracted a solemn vow from me not to share the secret of the precious metals within that forsaken mine, but if I was going to learn anything new, I had to share some of what I'd discovered. Whether Martha noticed my sigh or not I could not tell, but she listened intently as I said, 'Do you know why a company like the Bergmann Brothers might choose to hide the identities of their workers?'

'Hide?' She leaned conspiratorially against the bar, chin resting upon her knuckles. As I'd hoped, her curiosity had been piqued. 'Well, that is a bit strange. Could be some illegal workers that they didn't want anyone knowing about. Or…' Martha's eyes drifted toward empty space, as though a third participant had joined our conversation. 'No, that's just old rumors… mother was senile when she spouted on about that…'

'Rumors could still help,' I urged. Sweat trickled down the side of my face, brought on by a mixture of excited though cautious curiosity and the enduring heat. 'Especially if they're rumors linked to the mine.'

'Well…' Martha met my eyes again, and this time their darkness spoke of haunted memories. 'My ma was but a kid when the mine was closed—we're talking less than ten years old, but old enough to remember what people were saying—and she was good at sneaking into places she wasn't supposed to be. She'd laugh when she told us about her sneaking. She'd tell us the stories a hundred times, but she laughed every time.'

She sighed and drank a mouthful of the beer. 'Well, as she got older and her mind started to wander, she started to tell us new stories. Unpleasant stories. And when she told us these stories, she didn't laugh. She cried. She cried every time, and we'd have to wrap a blanket around her shoulders and…

'Ah, God, you don't need to know that. What she'd tell us, though, is that men would vanish in the mines. Poof! Gone. And then they'd reappear, except they weren't themselves. They'd be mad, wild eyes and everything, attacking whoever ran into them. Most of them were shot dead. Some of them went running off into the desert to feed the vultures. But ma swore to us that some of them got hidden away in secret cells beneath the jail… or was it the old doctor's place?

'She'd get confused a lot. She was old, y'know? Very old. She kept holding on for years, though, always refusing to leave this place. Said she belonged here; that Manhattan's secrets have to stay in Manhattan, and so she did, too.'

Martha sighed and chugged down the remainder of her beer whilst I sat in reserved silence.

Whether true or not, this recounting of her mother's rambles had added yet another layer to the mysteries of the mine. Not only was the mine abandoned despite a hoard of minerals waiting just a handful of pickaxe strikes away, but people were, supposedly, disappearing and going mad whilst it was still in operation. Was this the company's reasoning for closing down the dig? If so, what in the mines had elicited such sanity shattering effects? Furthermore, why cover up the identities of those who had been affected?

'Do you know of anyone else ever talking about secret cells?' I asked.

Martha shrugged. 'Sorry, can't say I ever have.' She poured more whiskey into my glass. 'Look, young man; these were the ramblings of a senile old woman. Stories of a fevered mind. Don't put too much stock in what I told you. As I said, probably just illegals who died, and they didn't want to face the consequences.'

'Well…' I downed the whiskey, and even watered down it burned my throat. 'Could you point me to anyone in particular who might know more? Anyone here, for example?'

'If you see someone with grey hair—or none—they're probably old enough to remember news about the mine. Back then, people cared about it, but now it's just a rocky reminder of why we're trapped here in the first place.' Though she appeared ready to walk away and be done with the subject, Martha hesitated a moment longer. 'You said you went to the town hall?' I nodded. 'Well, I'm sure you met Diana, then. Grey-haired old woman, thin as a twig? She should know plenty of stuff about the mine, being one of the councilors; her pa was one of the men in charge around here when the mine actually closed down.'

It was an unusual way to learn the name of someone you'd already met, but I was grateful for the information. Martha, though, was already putting some distance between us, though no one else was at the bar.

Diana could wait, I decided. Whilst I was here, it was worth attempting to find out what I could from the saloon's regulars. Though none had deigned to join me at the bar itself, they had secreted themselves in booths and at tables around the building.

Following Martha's advice, I sought out the grey-haired old folk of Manhattan, which appeared to be the majority of those who were present. By now most had turned away from me, taking little interest in the outcome of my conversation with their provider of inebriation; a few pairs of eyes still lingered, however, and it was to these individuals I went first.

The first individual I spoke with was a skeleton of a man, some eighty years old, whose sunken face spoke of decades spent drinking, smoking and almost starving. He was, unfortunately, nowhere near sober, slurring every word; this did not mean he was unwilling to share what he knew. Or rather, what he thought he knew.

According to this man, whose name was either Martin or Marvin, the mine was a death-trap. His father had worked there until it had suddenly been closed down, and would rant every day about madmen putting him out of a job. My unreliable storyteller cursed the Bergmann Brothers for closing the mine. 'They were scared of going mad like the poor miners they sent into the depths,' he spat, 'so they ran away as soon as the gold was gone.'

It wasn't much more to go on, but it did support Martha's ma's story about men going mad in the mine. As such, I shook Martin's—or Marvin's—hand and bought him another drink. He didn't need it, but I felt obliged to repay him somehow.

The next story I heard came from a trio seated around a corner table, who had been watching me listen to the drunkard's tale with such intensity that I had been certain a spider was circling my neck. They were far less intoxicated, though, and infinitely more coherent. All it took was the promise of a free drink and the information started flowing.

'I'll tell you this much,' the shriveled up little woman of the trio said. 'When that mine dried up, the company couldn't get out of here quick enough. Left all sorts behind in the mine. My aunt said something exploded in there not long after. The fools left dynamite behind, and something set it off one day. A miracle there wasn't a rockslide.'

The eldest of the two men at the table—brothers, they told me—shook his head the whole time. 'No, no, there was gases in that mine. That's why they left. Your aunt didn't see the people who would stumble into the doctor's house every day when their shifts ended. Our ma did; she was the nurse hereabouts. They'd come in with pounding headaches, coughing up green dust and moaning about rocks that moved. Gas! It was full of gas! That explosion would'a been a gas pocket being ignited.'

'Yeah, but by what?' the other brother asked. 'Maybe it was dynamite ignited the gas.'

'Oh, shut up,' the elder snapped. 'You're just backing her up because you're married to her...'

From there, the conversation devolved into an argument as to whether it was dynamite or gas in the mine, so I bid them farewell and moved to another table. There I sat in solitude, reflecting the philosophers of old as I pondered, stroking my chin with my elbow upon my knee.

More information, and yet the mystery grew. I couldn't be certain of the veracity of the stories I was being fed. They were little more than repeated rumors from individuals I understood to be dead. None of the people I could speak to in Manhattan were old enough to remember the mine when it was open, and even on the off-chance that one person in the entire town was that old, they would have been an infant and therefore of little more use than Martin—or Marvin—or the trio of squabbling siblings and in-laws.

The matter of madness, and guesses at gases, though, had given me new avenues of exploration.

Sitting alone at the shadow-soaked table at Martha's, I made a decision that would set me on a collision course with chaos. If I was going to find out whether events in the mine had scared the Bergmann Brothers out of Manhattan, I would have to check it out for myself.

I would have to enter the mine.

CHAPTER 5
DELVING INTO THE DEPTHS

Uncle Bert hadn't been lying when he said he still had some of my great-grandpa's gear at hand. If anything, he had been underselling the situation.

Upon disclosing my intention to enter the mine and determine if there was any truth to the tales told by Manhattan's drunkest and oldest, he had scrambled out of his chair and fervently insisted I join him on a walk into his back garden. It was a strikingly overgrown piece of land, without grass but coated in thorny, brown, sinister shrubs that snaked across the ground like barbed wire. He had, at some point, carved a path through them, leaving wicked barbs jutting out at ankle height, which proved challenging to avoid as we shuffled our way to an old, dilapidated shack at the far end of the yard.

Compared to this building, Bert's house was immaculate. One wall had fallen inward, held up only by a thick if warped wooden beam; where there had once been windows there were only dark voids fringed with jagged glass, and the door was little more than a plank of wood standing haphazardly against the entrance. This building had been built by great-grandpa Otto and had been dedicated entirely to the preservation of his equipment.

To my utter shock, despite its decrepit state, it had done just that. Within the shack, which I dared not enter myself, was a hefty chest the height of a man and the depth of two, and within that hefty standing chest was all my great-grandpa's equipment from his years in the mines.

Somehow, Bert managed to slide the chest out of the building, and though he was beyond breathless he seemed somewhat pleased with himself. Without words, he gestured to the great trunk; I approached it with hesitation, aware that insects and arachnids liked to lurk in shady places. What would come crawling out? Cockroaches? Scorpion?

I unclipped the thick leather straps, muscles tense, ready to pull my hands away as soon as anything touched me. A shaky breath broke from my lips as the buckle fell away; nothing fell into my hair as I pried the case open. I swore at myself for letting my imagination get away from me.

The interior was pristine, perhaps the only thing in all of Manhattan untainted by dust, though sandy swirls seemed to immediately seek entry. There were no cobwebs nor mothballs, and the equipment itself appeared free of dirt, the only signs of its use seen in the scratches upon metal and discoloration on the clothes.

It was the helmet that drew my attention first, typical miner's gear with the daintiest of dents at its peak. Holding it in my hand, I felt peculiarly connected to the great-grandpa I had never known nor heard stories about. This was a part of him, and that part of him bore a direct connection to the mystery I was confronting. I traced the small lamp that sat at the helmet's brim, cold to the touch, unused for almost a century.

Everything had been half-forgotten for years, just as Manhattan had, yet in this chest was the antithesis of the town. Whilst dust and degradation had settled in amongst the hopeless hearts of the people and the buildings left to crumble from the inside out, my great-grandpa's equipment had remained clean, strong and ready.

I took what I could carry from the chest. The sturdy pickaxe, the helmet, the overalls themselves, and even a stick of dynamite that had been squirrelled away in the back of the container. I was going to take up the lantern from the chest, too, but my uncle informed me he had a high-powered flashlight in the house that would serve me better.

Clad in all that gear, I looked like a man from the past, a relic of a bygone era, but I also felt better prepared for my intended quest. If I was going to delve into a forsaken, forbidden mine, I may as well look the part, after all.

My uncle grinned at me once I was dressed. 'Anyone sees you climbing up to the mine, they'll think you're a ghost,' he chuckled. 'Now off with you, boy. It's almost noon already, and you'll want to be out of there before dark so you can find your way out with the daylight. Oh, and one more thing.' He rummaged around the chest and drew out a thick coil of rope. 'Tie this to your belt, and then the other end to one of the posts outside the place. Should stop you getting lost, God willing.'

His cautious excitement proved contagious, and I found myself smiling back. Tying one end of the rope to my belt, and carefully wrapping the rest about my shoulder, I said, 'I'd invite you along, but I don't want to put you in any danger. If there's gas in there, I'll need to get out fast…'

'Don't you worry about it,' he replied, delivering a hearty slap to my shoulder. 'There's only gear enough for you, anyway, and I'd just get in the way. Just keep an eye out for any gold while you're digging up those secrets, eh?'

'Of course.'

***

The mine stared back at me with its lonely black eye as I lingered just beyond the threshold of the pit. Without my uncle's company, and with the stories of sanity shattering gases and reappearing madmen in mind, the very notion of entering those abandoned depths turned my blood into ice.

Add onto that the very real risk of a cave-in or encountering unseen animals that may have made the mine their home, I was beginning to reconsider my decision.

This, though, was why I had come to this forsaken, forgotten town. I reminded myself of that fact, overcoming the burgeoning desire to turn back. If I was going to uncover the story of this abandoned mine, I was going to have to go in. An expedition into the depths may not have been my original intention, but the mysteries I had uncovered could only, I was convinced, be answered by first-hand observation.

I felt compelled to discover if there was indeed still gold down there, and I was beyond curious to know if there was any truth to the rumors of gas. Asking questions would only get me more stories, and whilst speculative information was useful, it was nothing compared to true empirical data. If further questioning of the town's residents—specifically the two-person town council—was required, then I wanted to have facts to fall back on.

Following my uncle's suggestion, I tethered myself to one of the beams at the mine's entrance, taking deep, steadying breaths as I did. The darkness before me maintained its foreboding presence, like a wall warning me of my proximity to an inescapable abyss. I chased away its oppressive gaze with the light of my flashlight and plunged forth into the claustrophobic chasms of old Manhattan Mine.

Varying sensations struck me as I paced steadily into those depths. First and foremost was the tightness of the tunnels; how men worked side by side here in years long since passed, I could not fathom. Somehow carts of rock and mineral had rolled along the now rusted tracks, past scores of hard-working men, and yet for me it felt like the tunnel walls were mere inches from my skin. It did, though, give me some idea of how great-grandpa Otto had come by the dent on his helmet.

In those narrow conditions I was also keenly aware of the enveloping gloom, and the permeation of earthly smells around me, though it was difficult to place any one scent. At times I was sure I was surrounded by iron, at other times it was little more than a smell like warm soil on a summer's day;

there were pockets of air that stunk of coal, mud, and other smells I couldn't identify. I was grateful, though, that none of the scents struck me as gas.

Soon enough, I was shuffling along the tunnels to find my way. As I went, I passed broken pickaxes, their shafts eaten away, and abandoned lanterns that had long since burnt out. I didn't stop anywhere long to investigate, experiencing a weight upon my shoulders as though my body was all that stopped the mine from collapsing, always hoping the next tunnel I turned down would lead to an open cavern.

Beads of sweat formed and rippled on my skin, soaking through my shirt and into the overalls. The air in the mine was smothering, void of circulation, and hung around me like a cloud of flies. Every sixth step was accompanied by an exasperated sigh and a quick wiping of my brow, and again I wondered how the miners had worked down here, cramped in beside each other for hours at a time.

Was it really any wonder some of them went mad? Gas be damned.

Despite my discomfort, I pushed onwards, checking the rope at my waist as I went, and finding there was still some slack in it. The air cooled slightly as I moved deeper, brushing against my skin and making my sweat feel like tiny drops of ice. I shivered, and then came to a standstill.

The light of my flashlight reached far ahead, but no more than fifteen meters beyond me the tunnel suddenly stopped. A barrier of tumbled rocks barred further passage, and I swore at the detrimental turn of events. I would have to backtrack, returning to the hotter air back the way I had come. From there, I would follow another tunnel, taking a different route down into the depths of this abandoned Tartarus. I silently hoped the next passages I perused would lead to something of interest.

There had been nothing along this route except the aforementioned relics of long-abandoned digs.

I navigated the winding pathways of dug out earth, persistently fearing that the supports would crack as I passed them, as though a ripple in the air caused by my presence was all it would take to finally break them. My heartbeat echoed like a hundred drums in my head, the only sound in the empty darkness aside from my own tentative footsteps, and still I was no closer to making any discoveries or finding any answers.

At least ten times I found myself in tunnels that ended abruptly. One of them was boarded off at the end, but peering through this wooden barricade showed only a pile of jumbled rocks. Every time, it seemed, the air cooled just before I came up against another obstruction.

On one occasion I lingered in the cool air for a time, wondering whether this change of miniature climate was a by-product of whatever gas had supposedly seeped through the gloom. I did not smell anything out of the ordinary; taking time to test the air, I experienced no symptoms I would consider to be a sign of gas. No headaches, no dizziness, no coughing. In the end, I concluded it was probably just a sign of how deep I had walked, and the distance between myself and daylight.

Ultimately, I decided it would be worth trying one more tunnel and hoping it took me towards long buried answers. If I was led to another dead end, then it would be time to cut my losses and leave. It would be a disappointing outcome for myself and for Uncle Bert, though for two very different reasons. That wasn't to say, however, that there wouldn't be other opportunities.

Testing that the rope was still secure, and content in the knowledge that the flashlight's batteries still had plenty of life left, I plunged back into the depths of Manhattan Mine. My main hope as I debated which of the countless twists and turns to take was that I would find the route leading to the deepest parts of the mine. These would most likely be the last areas to be excavated, where the gloryholes of gold, silver and whatever other precious minerals the Bergmann Brothers sought could be found.

And perhaps clues as to the true reasons for the mine's abandonment.

The ground sloped steeper as I pursued my downward course, the supports appearing at increasingly frequent intervals overhead. The fear center of my mind screamed that this was a sign of instability ahead, but curiosity proved the louder motivator; I was moving deeper into the earth, toward answers, towards treasures of both mind and money.

Cool air greeted me, and my heart fluttered. Despairing thoughts worried that I would be faced by yet another wall of broken rocks and crumbling earth, but as I continued to delve down, down, down into the darkness of the underworld I was met by no such obstruction. Despair turned to hope. Hope became excitement.

And then the rope went taut, tugging me away from hell.

CHAPTER 6
DIGGING UP DESPAIR

The strangled shout that burst from my chest was three parts surprise, two parts frustration, and one-part exhaustion. After walking for so long, my feet aching and forehead soaked, I had finally found a passage leading to the deepest depths of the mine, only for the rope to run short. My hopelessness was washing away, but now, as the rope fought to drag me back toward the light above, it started to creep back in.

My eyes watered, and I honestly could not tell whether this was a product of misery, or the shock of my belt biting into my hip.

I swore to myself and muttered half-hearted curses at my uncle for not providing me with more rope. To be halted now felt unfair, as the tunnel winded on ahead of me, even the flashlight not powerful enough to illuminate it in its entirety. How much further did it go? What waited beyond?

Untethering myself would be madness. Turning back, though, was an action I was entirely unwilling to undertake. Not after all the dead ends and obstructions I had encountered up until now. Here was a passage that led into the deepest reaches of Manhattan Mine, and it was in those depths I felt certain I would find answers. Would it not, after all, have been in these final, cavernous passageways that the Bergmann Brothers encountered whatever strange circumstances had forced them to close the mine with such suddenness?

Swearing again in hushed whispers, I untied the rope from my belt and wrapped it around the nearest beam it could reach. As long as I could find my way back here, then I would be able to navigate my way to the surface. The path ahead appeared to be somewhat straightforward.

My first steps into the cool gloom ahead were tentative, my mind plagued by concerns that this decision would be the end of me. I pushed on. The flashlight illuminated the shored-up tunnels, the supporting beams present every handful of steps. How much earth was above my head? Something cold clawed its way up my back at the question; I turned my thoughts back to my current undertaking.

The slope of the forsaken tunnel led me further down, and now the earth began to stink of something fetid, not unlike the rotting of a roadside carcass. My assumptions of animals entering the mine must have been correct, though apparently they had not thrived as expected. Rumors of gas returned to the forefront of my mind as I fought not to gag at the growing stench.

Had the animals fallen victim to it, too?

Changes in the geology of the earth around me began to occur as I delved ever deeper, becoming the focus of my flashlight's light. Signs of the digging of man faded out to be replaced by natural formations of jagged rock. Along the way, some sections had been dug out, becoming a hybrid of mine and cave, but before long it seemed I was walking in an entirely wild and primeval system, long buried and unknown to mankind or its ancestors.

I found myself wondering how far into these caves the miners had dared to tread. By now, all signs of man's intrusion had disappeared; I was accompanied only by the ever growing, throat burning odor of rot and decay, though there was nothing in sight to suggest the recent presence of any living thing.

Ahead of me, the rocky passage twisted to the right, illuminated not just by my flashlight, but by an eerie green glow from sources unknown. I was familiar with subterranean, bioluminescent fungi due in no small part to a friend I had made at university. We were studying entirely different majors, but chance had seen us brought together by a common interest in cryptology. Even the knowledge imparted by our companionship did little to lessen the frightful effect of the ethereal light.

What must the miners have thought if they delved this far?

The closer I got to the ghostly glow, the stronger the smell of decay became. Covering my mouth, still lacking a definite source of the smell, I worried whether this was actually the gas the townsfolk had spoken of. Aside from the throat-burning stench, however, I didn't feel like I was encountering any side effects. Especially none that could be regarded as maddening.

When I rounded the corner, I finally came face to face with the source. I hadn't been wrong when I theorized that some animals had gotten lost and expired in this peculiar pit. At first it was only bones, broken and half-buried, littered across the rocky ground. Then I started to see pieces of flesh, rotted and ravaged, some clinging to bone, remnants of beasts unrecognizable. It seemed the further along that sickening, subterranean graveyard I walked, the less decayed the remains became. Piled upon yet more bones and shredded carcasses, halfway between mummification and putrescence, were the corpses of coyotes, reptiles, rodents, and even some sheep.

These heaps of death appeared to terminate just outside of a man-sized opening that led into what I could already see was an expansive chamber. This chamber, it transpired, was also the source of the grotesquely green glow.

There were no flies to pester me, but the malodorous decomposition left me almost unable to breathe. Even taking in air through my mouth alone plagued me with the taste of expired meat, every organ fighting not to violently protest at the injustices being done to them. The acidic bile that rose into my mouth was almost a welcome alternative, were it not accompanied by the torturous twisting of my stomach.

My previously cautious footsteps became a scramble for the ghastly lit chamber, putting some level of distance between myself and the accumulation of corruption I had stumbled across. Even in the creepy cavern, the fetid odor remained strong, but I was no longer also undergoing the assault upon my vision. In my rush to escape the sickening sight, I had been sure I'd seen a human skull amidst the despoiled debris; it was likely just my imagination, I assured myself, but the notion still lingered.

Once my labored breathing had returned to normality, and my stomach had tired of its somersaults, I assessed my newfound surroundings. It was, I soon realized, no surprise that the foul stench yet lingered, for this cavern's only opening was the one through which I had entered. Jagged rocks formed an imperfectly spherical wall around the disconcerting cave, coated in curious, bioluminescent lichen-like growths. The curvature of the chamber terminated in a series of stalactites oddly concentrated almost exclusively at the room's center, without stalagmite twins below. Instead, they hung above an almost perfectly cubic rock that must have been hewn from the ground centuries, or even millennia ago, though how it had come to be in this closed-off, organic yet somehow unnatural formation I could not begin to explain.

Though I am by no means a geologist, it was impossible not to see that this rock was of a sort entirely different to that which surrounded me. In all of the mine I had come across little that was not brown, be it light as sand or dark as soaked clay; this odd stone was grey, marbled by faded greens and black-tinted reds. Truthfully, I had never seen the like.

Curiosity, mercifully, broke through the pallor of revulsion that had plagued me since discovering this seemingly unexcavated, oddly alien section of the mine. The fetor forgotten, I knelt before the out-of-place object and ran my hand across its surface.

Its top was smooth, like a perfectly polished table, yet the sides and front remained rough. Upon closer inspection it also seemed that tools had been used to mark the rock, forming odd somewhat runic impressions, entirely unfamiliar—though perhaps recognizable to students of linguistics or occultism, only one of whom I could hazard to call a friend.

My proximity highlighted something else I had not initially noticed. At the front edge of the rock was a narrow gap, so small a coin would barely fit into it. Finding a use for my great-grandpa's pickaxe for the first time on this curious expedition, I dug out some of the ground around and under the strange slab. This revealed a pit, swathed in shadow, which appeared to descend deep into the earth below. My curiosity became a feverish determination to uncover the secrets of this mysterious section of the mine; I was overwhelmed by the notion that something here was responsible for the mine's closing, and perhaps even the madness induced in the temporarily missing miners.

Resting upon my stomach, flashlight waiting at my side, I peered into the tenebrous chasm. Objects far below sparkled like stars, reflecting the indirect light that touched them now for the first time in at least a century. My heart raced; here was one of the glory-holes the Bergmann Brothers had uncovered, I was certain of it.

Grabbing the flashlight, I inclined its light toward the pitch-black pit. A split second later, I scrambled away, hand over my mouth as my stomach resumed the acrobatic performance it had practiced outside the cavern.

In that pit, packed in amongst the lustrous metals embedded in the earth, I saw piled upon each other the unblemished, methodically polished, flesh-forsaken skulls of human beings, surrounded by similarly spotless bones of a size and shape consistent with the skeletons of men. I retched as I stumbled around the cave, my vision blurred, unbalanced by the shocking sight. Rotten rodents, reptiles and desert beasts I could somewhat handle, but to see the ritualistic treatment of these remains shook my soul to its core.

Falling to my knees knocked the air from my lungs, and my next intake of breath was accompanied by a horrific, gurgled sob. Was this, then, the sinister secret of Manhattan Mine? Men, murdered by maddened miners they had once called friends; murdered, skinned and fed unto the darkness below.

Incoherent as I was, I could not fathom what would drive men to such dark depravities.

A chill grabbed hold of me, dancing on my sweat-soaked skin. No longer was I enthusiastically exploring the scandalous history of a long-abandoned mine. Now I had uncovered crimes so heinous I would be accused of fantasy were I ever to record what had been concealed in these depths for so long.

Damning myself for ever setting out on this search, I wiped the tears from my eyes with shaking hands, ignoring the piercing pain in my skull, like needles pressing upon my brain. My legs fought against my need to stand, but I swore and forced myself to my feet. Though I stumbled, I stood, bracing myself against the green-glowing walls, ignoring the tingling in my toes. Snatching the flashlight and pickaxe from their place beside the abyss, I lurched back toward the dreadful doorway that had permitted my entry to this cursed cave and half-sprinted, half-scrambled back toward the man-made tunnels I had so foolishly thought to explore.

Uncle Bert would be pleased to know there was indeed still gold in the mine; I laughed to myself with venom at the thought. If he dared to brave the damned depths of this most unholy of hells, then he could have it all. Damn him. Damn him for encouraging me.

By some bizarre prescience I found my way back to the beam and the rope I had so recklessly left behind, wishing to myself that I had turned back then and accepted my failure for the day. Now my mind was haunted by the horror I had witnessed, and the realization of its ramifications.

I did not stop to rest, nor to tether myself to the rope again. Instead, I trudged my way through the winding tunnels, now oddly comforting, as my adrenaline seeped away and exhaustion overcame me. The pain in my head lingered, and I wondered whether I had struck it upon anything despite great-grandpa Otto's helmet; my vision remained blurry, my breathing was labored, and the rotten fetor lingered still in my nose and mouth.

At last, I saw light ahead of me, and hurried out of the malevolent mine, allowing my legs to buckle only once I was beyond the terrible threshold and back upon the rocky ridge.

The light I had seen was not the sunlight, however. Instead, it was the silver glow of a full moon, hanging low in a cloudless sky. Stars, true stars, shone like beacons in the night, promising me safety from the nightmare I had left behind. The desert shimmered like a silver sea, and the town became ethereal ships, and for that brief instant I was far, far away from the mysteries of Manhattan Mine.

I did not look behind me. I did not try to stand. I simply closed my eyes, surrounded by the chilled air of desert night, and escaped from the nightmare that lurked below.

CHAPTER 7
AN INTERROGATION INVERTED

I woke from my feverish sleep slumped over in Uncle Bert's armchair. Muted sunlight streaked through the dusty window, striking my face, the heat like a hot iron upon my skin. Dry-mouthed, and nursing a skull-squeezing headache, I stirred in the seat and leant out of the light.

My most burning concern was just how, exactly, I'd come to be back in my uncle's house. Had he climbed the entire way up that hill, with little but moonlight to show the way? Or had I, in a fugue state, shambled down myself?

As though my waking had summoned him, Bert shuffled into the living room, two steaming cups of coffee in hand. 'I was just about to wake you,' he grumbled, resting the cups on the skewed table. Taking a seat across from me, I noticed his red-rimmed, baggy eyes. 'You weren't back before dark like I told you to be, so I started to worry. It would be just typical that as soon as someone wanders into that mine it would collapse in on you. Glad to see that wasn't the case.' He chuckled and grabbed his drink. Taking a sip, he hissed at the heat and set it back down. 'Looks like there was some truth to the gas stories, though, eh? Or did you just bump your head particularly hard?'

Leaning forward, eager for some degree of hydration, I grasped my coffee and took one tongue-burning mouthful. I was able to somewhat overcome the pain, but, like my uncle, found I had to put the drink back down. 'I'm not entirely sure what happened. I went pretty deep, to a point where the miners must have dug, or blasted, into a natural cave. I found… something. Something awful. I ran from it as fast as I could, and as soon as I was out of there I collapsed, and that was it.'

'Found something?' Bert asked. 'Found… what?'

I took a slow breath, my mouth still dry despite the coffee, and my mind still reeling, still attempting to piece together what exactly I'd witnessed in that malicious mine. Unsure how to explain it, I gave my uncle a full recount of the initial expedition. He nodded along, impatient, as I described the dead ends with their cooler air, and the numerous tunnels I'd travelled down. He appeared almost to be dropping off when I finally returned to the subject of the cave, at which point he grabbed his coffee and leant forward in his seat.

When I completed my spine-chilling account, we sat in silence, both our faces drawn of blood. Revisiting the subject had chased away the fog that obscured my memories; vivid images of that pit of bones, and the rotting, spoiled carcasses piled beyond the chamber flashed in my mind. My stomach twisted, and I had to fight the urge to sprint from the room and vomit.

Uncle Bert was similarly disturbed, though he had not seen what I had seen. There was, however, something he *had* seen that I did not.

'When I found you up there,' he explained, eyes cast into the swirls of his cold coffee, 'you were sprawled out across the ground. But there was a green mist around you. I just thought it was a bit of dust, colored strange by some odd moonlight effect, but...' He shook his head, and when he put the cup down, I thought I saw his hands trembling. 'Maybe my imagination is wandering a bit after what you just told me—God... bones in a pit—but I'm sure that same mist, or dust, or whatever it was, was gathered around the entrance to the mine.'

'Gas,' I muttered. Had I somehow released whatever sanity-sapping element the miners encountered down there?

'I'm sure what you saw is real,' Bert said, leaning back in his seat. 'But don't discount the possibility that whatever I saw clinging to you was messing with your head.'

I nodded, though my hands clenched at the suggestion. He was right; if there was gas down there, then I could have easily been hallucinating. Deep within, though, I was absolutely certain there had been no trickery involved.

There were human bones buried down there.

The silence that had settled between us was suddenly disturbed by a hefty knock on Bert's front door, startling us. Heart hammering, I watched as Bert rose from his seat and shuffled toward the lobby.

My ears were struck by the awful creak of the door as Bert inched it open; what he said next did little to settle my heartbeat. 'Ah, Councilwoman, this is unexpected.'

I was on my feet in an instant, shrugging off great-grandpa Otto's overalls and stuffing them unceremoniously behind Bert's chair. I could barely hear what was being said, but I was able to make out three voices: Uncle Bert, the ashen lady from the town hall, and the deep tones of someone I'd never met.

'... suppose you'd best come on in, then,' Bert said. Limping his way back into the living room, he led two individuals in after him. One was Councilwoman Diana, the other a mustachioed man in weathered jeans and a tucked in blue polo shirt; both bore the same red-rimmed, baggy eyes of people who haven't slept. 'Max, this is Diana, but I believe you've met.'

'We have,' the grey-haired twig of woman said, presenting me with an unfriendly half-smile. 'You haven't met our Sheriff yet, though, have you?'

The unknown man smiled at me and stretched out a hand. 'Pleasure to meet you, Max.' I returned the handshake, his grip making my bones ache. 'I'm the only police presence you'll find around here.'

'So... do I just call you Sheriff, then?' I asked, as the four of us sat ourselves down.

'Funny story there,' the man said; whilst he chuckled, Diana rolled her eyes and folded her arms. 'My pa had a bit of a sense of humor, y'see. He decided my future before I was even born.' Bert and Diana said nothing, sitting in uncomfortable silence. The man sighed. 'My name's Sheriff. Sheriff Sheriff of Manhattan.'

'If it's alright with you,' I replied, smiling despite the tension building in the small, dark, dusty room, 'I'll just call you Sheriff.'

He laughed at that and nodded. 'That'll be just fine, kid.'

'The reason we're here,' Diana snapped, cutting through Sheriff's laughter, 'is to check in on your wellbeing. There was some strangeness around town last night. People said they saw dark shapes moving around on the ridge, which then disappeared into a mist that... what were people saying?'

'Disappeared into a green mist that drifted towards the moon,' Sheriff finished.

'Yes, exactly that,' Diana continued. 'The Matthews tell me they had some frightful nightmares last night, and so did a few other families hereabouts. The Barker boy brings you food sometimes, right?' Bert nodded but was given no opportunity to speak. 'Well, he's supposedly been screaming all day, Mary Barker says, because he had the same nightmare.'

'Nightmares?' I asked. 'Shared ones?'

'Yeah, all dreaming the same awful stuff,' Sheriff replied. His expression betrayed a certain uneasiness around the subject. 'Something about a rock covered in skulls, and...' He shivered. 'And skin hanging from hooks.'

Uncle Bert stared at me, long and hard. *'Did you see anything like that?'* his eyes seemed to ask. My own dreams from the night before were nothing more than blurry afterimages; thinking of them, however, left me nervous. I suppressed a shudder, wondering what terrors I had unleashed.

Diana, seemingly unaware of my uncle and I's discomfort, continued. 'Did either of you happen to see anything last night? This house is one of the closest to the mine.'

'I don't tend to look up there much,' Bert replied with an unconvincing shrug. 'Besides, I can't see much through my windows.'

Diana's eyes turned toward me; her brow creased into a frown that made her entire face appear skull-like. 'And what about you? You've been digging around town lately, asking questions about the mine.' Her voice became unpleasantly accusatory. 'Do you happen to know anything?'

'I'm not sure I like your tone,' Uncle Bert half-snarled. 'He may be an outsider, but he's still my nephew.' Diana folded her arms, unbothered. 'I'm not sure I want you in my house right now.'

'No, no, it's okay,' I said. Though it seemed I was being interrogated, I recognized the opportunity I had been presented with. Leaning forward in my seat, I dared to meet Diana's steely eyes, noting the dark rings beneath them. 'You seem particularly disturbed by whatever is going on at the mine,' I broached. 'Is there something I should know about it?'

'For starters,' Sheriff replied, his somewhat cheery, if tired, expression giving way to a scowl, 'it's off-limits. Public safety and all that. There shouldn't be anyone up there, and everyone around here knows it. Beyond that... well...'

'It's off-limits,' Diana repeated. Her gaze was intense, and it took all my willpower not to look away. 'That's all you need to know.'

'I'm starting to think there's something else going on here.' I adjusted my position in the seat, leaning forward with my elbows upon my knees. 'Everyone I've talked to has suggested they're *unable* to leave; they don't want to stay here, but they have to.'

'Where are they meant to go?' Diana scoffed. 'They don't have money, and they don't know anyone outside of this town. Don't look too far into that, Mister Wolfe. It's just a shared sentiment amongst this town's unfortunate souls.'

'Now, now, wait a minute,' Sheriff said, stroking his snowy moustache. His face softened. 'Plenty of folk say this place won't let them go. Take the Kellers; they've got family in California who have said many a time that they'll help them out and give them a place to stay. Hell, they've packed up their house three times and tried to leave, but as soon as they start driving down that poor excuse of a road that leads away from here, they freeze up, turn around and moan about Manhattan refusing to let them go.

'You remember how I went with them the second time? It was a strange day, that; we stopped at the same time, without a word, without a signal. We just... couldn't drive any further.' He shrugged. 'Not to say that some folks just don't have the funds for it, but there's... there's definitely something strange about it.'

Hope surged in my heart. Whilst Diana seemed particularly reticent about discussing the town and the mine—despite her earlier willingness to let me peruse the records room—Sheriff seemed far more candid. 'That's not all I've heard,' I said, pursuing this opening as far as it would take me. 'There are stories of people going mad in that mine; something about gas.'

'So, you're the one who's been filling folks' heads with nonsense,' Diana hissed, lurching to her feet. 'I might have known. I never should have let you look at the town's records. I'd hoped that would be enough to satisfy your curiosity, but now you're making wild speculations about madmen in the mine—'

'Sit down!' Bert's voice was stronger than I'd heard all week, his exhausted eyes full of fire. 'Don't pretend that people don't whisper about such things. It's been the main topic of gossip around here as long as I can remember. There was weirdness afoot in the mine before it closed. My grandpa always said so. Don't pretend you don't know nothing about it.'

'He's right, Di,' Sheriff said, watching her as she shrank back into the seat. 'Folk are always whispering about the mine. They know it's closed down for the sake of public safety, but they're not worried about collapsing beams or anything like that. They're worried about the gas.'

'There was never any evidence of gas,' Diana protested. 'You read the records, Mister Wolfe, and would have seen for yourself that there was *never* any evidence of gas.'

'Incomplete records,' I retorted, 'with expunged names.'

She sighed, evidently defeated. Sheriff, it seemed, had swung around to our side, if there were such a thing. 'Yes, okay, there were some... disappearances. My pa told me everything he knew about the mine before I took over from him. About *why* the Bergmann Brothers abandoned it. Some people went mad, there were some... incidents. Workers felt unsafe, and started to refuse to work, so they packed up and left.'

'Wait...' Sheriff turned in his seat, eyebrow cocked. 'I thought it ran dry. That's what we've always been told.'

'There's still gold down there,' I blurted, overcome by the revelations I was being drip-fed. Bert scowled at me, our promise shattered. Did it really matter, though? The Councilwoman already knew, and no doubt was about to say as much. 'It had nothing to do with the money, really. Whatever madness was going on down there, the Bergmanns didn't know how to handle it so made their escape before things got worse. No doubt the councilors at the time backed them up to avoid a panic.'

'You're right.' Diana's eyes dropped, staring into the worn, fraying fibers of Uncle Bert's carpet. A century of guilt fell upon her shoulders right before our eyes. 'But there's more.' We watched her; I was perhaps the most fascinated of us all, barely on my seat anymore. 'One of the miners is still alive...'

CHAPTER 8
THE MADMAN OF MANHATTAN

'I can't believe you've kept this a secret for all these years,' Sheriff grumbled as he steered the beaten-up old car along Manhattan's decaying streets. 'From me, especially, but did you never think the town deserved to know?'

I was sat in the back of the car, feeling like a prisoner despite the destination we had in mind. Silence, I found, was providing me with more information than a continuation of my questioning.

'About what?' Diana asked, staring out the clouded window. 'The mine not being dry, or the insane miner my grandpa locked up under the clinic?'

'Locked up?' Sheriff cried. The car swerved slightly. 'This just keeps getting worse…'

'Either way, people would have panicked,' the Councilwoman continued. 'It was better for everyone just to say the mine went dry. Grandpa thought everyone would just leave, and that would be it, but…'

'But that damn mine is keeping them here somehow,' Sheriff concluded, tutting to himself. 'Is there actually any gas, then, or was that a fabrication too?'

Diana tapped at the dashboard. 'There... there was never any *proof* of gas, but... well, it had to be something. People went down into that mine and came out... different.'

'Different?' I asked. 'How?'

'You'll understand when you see him,' she replied.

As soon as she had revealed the miner's existence, I had demanded to meet him. That had been met with a firm rebuke until Sheriff echoed me. Diana may not have been willing to show me, but it was clear to me that she couldn't say no to the lawman.

'You're going to explain this to me right now.' His words had been little more than a growl.

Diana sighed, glanced at me, then back to Sheriff. 'Fine. We'll go there and you can see why he's there.'

'And I'm coming with you,' I said, crossing my arms. 'Or should I start telling this town about the gold?' Of course, I had no real intention of sharing this information; this was my discovery, after all, and I couldn't have the locals destabilizing the mine with their tramping feet. But she didn't know that.

Perhaps realizing that she couldn't risk her citizens taking foolish forays into the darkness of Manhattan Mine, she acceded. No doubt she thought there was no other option available to her after her revelation. Bert refused to join us, claiming he needed some more sleep. It was only then that it occurred to me how exhausted he must be after carrying me all the way down the ridge.

Despite this, I was glad to have the opportunity; my uncle deserved some peace and quiet. This long-lived miner may have been mad, but surely he would be able to provide the final pieces of this particularly perplexing puzzle.

The clinic was a short distance from the town hall but blended in with all the buildings around it. It was a white-painted, single-story structure, resembling the ranch houses in Western movies. There was no clear sign that it was, indeed, a clinic at all, except for a small metal plaque nailed beside the door.

'Does the sky look a little odd to you?' Sheriff asked as he climbed out of the car. He opened the back door for me; stepping out, I gazed up and realized something did seem... off.

There was a subtle rippling to the usually matte blue heavens, which did not appear as vibrant as usual. There was the faintest of green tints, too, and that realization alone sent an icy chill up my spine.

'Let's just get inside, shall we?' Diana barked, leading the way.

The interior of the clinic was clean but empty, perhaps one of the only places in the entire town that wasn't caked in dust. A simple wooden desk was set to one side of the spacious room we entered, with a single, dented metal filing cabinet beside it. A young woman sat at that desk, watching us enter with a bemused expression on her face.

Beyond this desk, I could see two simple beds with wooden side tables. On the other side of the room were a pair of doors. One was a toilet; the other was marked with a small sign reading "Consultations". This seemed to be the extent of the clinic's provisions, and I was quietly glad I hadn't been injured in the mine.

'Good morning, Doctor Wilson.' Sheriff nodded his head to the building's lone occupant. 'How are things?'

'I've had a few people come in this morning complaining of unusual headaches and a sleepless night, but otherwise it's been quiet,' she replied. 'Is everything okay?' Her eyes darted between the sheriff and myself, and then lingered on Diana. 'Councilwoman? Is something wrong?'

'Everything's fine,' Diana replied, her voice possessing the same sharpness that had characterized her visit to Bert's house. 'We're going to need to use the consultation room.'

Doctor Wilson glanced at the room in question, then shrugged. 'Sure, I haven't got any appointments lined up. Do you need any help with anything?'

'No, we'll be fine.' Diana gestured for Sheriff and I to follow her; Sheriff mouthed an apology to the doctor, and then we followed the frustrated Councilwoman into the room.

She locked the door behind us.

It was a modest little room, containing another bed and a pair of wooden chairs. There was a metal, glass-fronted cabinet on one side of the room containing various medicines, most of them in short supply, and a lone window which Diana crossed to, covering it with a curtain.

It was, overall, a rather plain room, but I considered I shouldn't have been surprised. I was, however, wondering why we'd come *here*. How were we meant to reach the madman from this room? My unasked question was answered when Diana produced a key from her pocket, which she inserted into an almost invisible slot in the wooden wall backing the bathroom.

Something clicked, and wooden panels popped away from the wall, revealing a carefully hidden door. Sheriff released an astounded gasp, whilst I simply cocked an eyebrow. When the door was swung open, the both of us winced at the stale air that surged out of the space behind it.

'Down here,' Diana instructed us with a sigh, disappearing into a dark, narrow space within the wall.

Sheriff indicated I should go first, so I followed Diana into the hidden passage. It was choked up with cobwebs, and descended immediately into a stone-walled, subterranean chamber. The smell that drifted up from this secret section of the clinic made me cough, my throat going dry; it was a vile combination of damp, waste, and rot.

Reaching the bottom of the short staircase, I found myself in a poor imitation of a medieval dungeon. Admittedly, the walls appeared clean, unblemished by moss in such a dry locale, but the gloom and mustiness that surrounded me made my skin crawl.

A set of metal bars split the room in half at the middle, and on the other side of those bars sat an emaciated, leathery excuse of a man. Truthfully, he looked like a mummified corpse, and for a moment I wondered whether the Councilwoman was the mad one here; then he blinked at me, and his chapped lips split into a rotted-toothed smile.

'God almighty,' Sheriff swore from behind me. 'He looks half-dead. This... this just isn't right.'

'The son of a bitch is over a hundred-and-twenty years old,' Diana countered. 'Of course he looks half-dead. He just refuses to die.'

'A pleasure to see you too,' the imprisoned madman rasped, almost unmoving. His voice reminded me of stone on steel, sending an unpleasant twitch down my back. 'I see you've brought guests this time. Are your forefathers' secrets coming back to bite you?'

His eyes fixed on me with an unnerving intensity, which was almost enough to chase me away from this dreadful chamber. 'I can tell you're not one of the local folks,' he remarked with a hateful sneer. 'Is this dreadful place finally back on the map? Oh, I certainly hope so. There's still gold, and silver, and even diamonds, I'm sure, down in those tunnels. Time to dig them up. Dig, dig, dig them up.'

'Nothing of the sort,' Diana growled.

The skeletal figure scoffed. 'Disappointing.'

'Councilwoman, this is just plain inhumane,' Sheriff cried, pointing at the man. 'What grounds do you have for imprisoning him?'

'Oh, she has plenty,' the madman chuckled. He climbed to his feet, bones creaking, skin taut. A flaky tongue darted out to wet his cracked lips. 'It just wouldn't be proper to let a killer like me wander the streets. Oh, the skins I would wear; the hearts I would eat; the bones I would gather.'

I recalled the supposed shared nightmares of the night before and shuddered.

'I still remember the cracking of skulls on stone, and the screams of the miners as I cut their friends' throats. Oh, the rush was like nothing you've ever known,' the man continued, grinning. 'One day I'll be back out there. Just you wait. You think a hundred years of incarceration will stop me? You could hold me for a thousand years, and I'll still be waiting.'

Councilwoman Diana rolled her eyes at the lunatic's rant. 'See, he's absolutely mad. Wearing skins... there's no proof he ever did it, but it's clear that's what he wants.'

'Why didn't they just kill him?' I asked. The madman turned his eyes onto me with a burning ferocity. 'If he was that dangerous, why not just kill him and make it look like an accident?'

Sheriff appeared appalled at the idea, his mouth falling open. Diana merely shrugged.

'Maybe they should have,' she said. 'But I can promise you I won't get my hands dirty like that. He's going to die in this cell, and that's the end of it.'

Those horrible, hateful eyes continued to linger on me; I turned my own to meet them. Unblinking, he sniffed the air between us. Suddenly the madman's brows raised, as if in sudden realization. 'Oh. Oh, oh, oh... I like you. Yes, let me speak with you. Alone. Just you.'

Sheriff stepped toward the bars. 'You shut up. I don't know what's going on here, but your shouting isn't helping anyone.'

'Let me speak with you,' the desiccated man pleaded. 'You want truth, and you have seen some of it. I'll tell you more. Oh, let me speak.' He spat towards the Councilwoman. 'Get out, get out, I want to speak only to him.'

Diana stepped up beside me and placed a hand on my shoulder, as though about to lead me away. The madman threw himself against the bars, pressing his leathery, fissured face between them. A glance at him, and then Diana muttered, 'You have five minutes. Then you come out and never speak of this again.'

I nodded, and they left me alone with the madman of Manhattan.

CHAPTER 9
ARE YOU SURE YOU WANT TO KNOW?

'Well… it's just us now,' I said, folding my arms.

His rotting teeth turned his grinning maw into a black pit of fetor. 'What did you see?' he hissed, eyes bulging. 'Tell me, what did you see in the darkness?'

I glanced toward the concrete steps that had led into this prison and was grateful that Diana and Sheriff were nowhere to be seen. Stepping cautiously closer to those bars, I whispered, 'I saw the pit of bones.' His grin, somehow, grew wider. 'Was that you, you sick bastard?'

A howling laugh escaped his throat. 'I knew it. I knew you'd been to the mine. I can smell it on you. Oh, you inquisitive soul, you just had to know what was down there, didn't you?' Stepping away from the bars, he paced around the cell, hard-soled feet slapping on the cold surface. 'You're just like the Bergmann Brothers, you know. Greedy. Greedy as man can be. Except you're not greedy for wealth; you're greedy for knowledge. Is that why you came to this hellhole? To learn?'

I frowned at the manic, prowling figure in front of me. 'This wasn't what I came looking for. I just wanted to understand what happens to towns like this when mines close, and to understand what kept them here. That cave, you, the mystery and the murders... that's not what I wanted.'

'And you're only just now scratching the surface.' He stopped, his head turning as though on a rusted hinge. 'Shall I tell you more? I can give you all the answers; what we found, all the names those Bergmann bastards erased, and why people stay. Just ask, friend. Just ask.'

I hesitated, the bars the only obstacle between us, aware that time was ticking silently away. He was mad, yes, but even madness carries some semblance of truth. Depending on what he told me now, I could extrapolate the facts later. Daring not to step any closer to the bars, I beckoned him closer; he approached like a dog desperate for attention. 'Alright. Tell me.'

His jaw popped as he smiled at me, eyes alight. Gnarled fingers wrapped around the bars, tongue darting over his lips as though to wet them, yet he only succeeded in freeing flakes of dead flesh. 'It was just a normal mine to start with. Everyone did their digging, retrieved the gold, and silver, and diamonds, and we kept going deeper, and deeper, and deeper. People would get headaches, but no one much cared because we were getting rich. Not as rich as the Bergmann Brothers, but rich nonetheless. Then someone blasted a bit of rock, and it revealed a cave. A natural cave. Well, the Brothers were excited by that finding. They were convinced there would be even more valuable rocks down there;

they sent a surveyor, and he said it was rife with precious metals. So suddenly we're all digging in the caves instead of the tunnels we'd worked so hard to shore up.

'Well, soon enough, another cave was found, but it was... weird. There was a strange smell in there, and once we found it, we started to notice animals would keep creeping inside. They'd wander down to that chamber we opened, and just lay down and die. Rumors went around about gas in the mine, and eventually the Bergmann Brothers sent someone to investigate.

'That was me. That was my job. They sent me down with a canary, and said if there was gas, I had to tell them where it was. Except the canary just kept tweeting, even once I went into the chamber. It was fine. So, I looked around, but I tripped over a rock and crushed the canary in its cage. Poor little canary...'

He stopped and sighed. Despite his words, however, a sickly smile creased his leathery face. After another second or so, he continued.

'Well, blood was what it wanted. The blood splashed on the stone, and it moved, revealing a pit. An empty pit of blackness. Well, I looked in that pit, and it looked right back at me. Something growled from down there, so I turned and ran. When the Brothers asked what happened, I told them the truth. Well, except for the pit. Somehow, I knew they wouldn't believe me if I told them about the pit.'

He stopped and stared at me, as though that was the end of the story. No doubt the other workers would have wished it all ended there, but we both knew it didn't.

'And?' I pressed him. 'What else happened?'

'I heard it whispering to me. It begged me to return,' the madman replied, clapping his hands. 'I went back down there, and I looked into the pit, and it spoke to me. It asked for bones, lots of bones, all the bones I could bring it. But not animals, no. It had enough animal bones. It needed the bones of men, now. I started to kill, to gather, and I threw those bones into the pit. Soon it only wanted skulls, so I would steal the heads of the miners and throw them down.

'After a while, others started to hear the whispers. They gave themselves willingly, or they ran away. Hoping to save face, the Bergmanns bribed all the right people to make sure those names disappeared. But the ones who ran... heh... they never left Manhattan either. It held them here, whispering to them. Many died in the desert, trying to flee but never getting far. It holds their kin too, though they cannot hear it. Only I was allowed to stay alive, because I gave it what it wanted, and did all the rituals it demanded. It filled my head with images, and I painted them on the walls in the blood of my victims; it commanded me to wear their skin as cloaks, so I did.

'Now you've gone and gazed into the pit. You dug too deep, just like the Bergmanns, and now everyone will face its wrath. Something stared back at you; you woke it up again. Events have been set in motion than cannot be undone. They tried to stop it before, they tried to bury it with their explosives, but it stole them away and ate it all.

'That's why the mine is closed. That's why there's still gold down there. It belongs to something older than time, though, and it wants to break free. It will be free, I promise you. It will. And I will stand before its glory, chosen to serve, whilst the rest of you crumble before its might!'

I didn't even hear Diana's footsteps as she charged down the steps. A moment later, she grabbed me by the collar of my shirt and dragged me out of that awful dungeon. My feet flailed on the steps, and it was a challenge not to fall, overpowered by the Councilwoman's grip.

***

Diana slammed the door closed, muting the ravings of the madman. 'Are you happy now?' she spat. 'Bloody lunatic, maybe I should just kill him.' She winced at the withering glare she received from Sheriff. 'I just hope you're satisfied now, Mr. Wolfe.' She shook her head, her eyes heavy. 'Take whatever that monster said with a pinch of salt, though, you hear? He was a killer, yes, but beheadings, wearing the skins of his victims... none of that was ever proven.'

She shuffled toward the office door and unlocked it. 'Be on your way, now,' she commanded. 'Finish up whatever you came here to do, and then leave us be. You've caused enough trouble in Manhattan.'

Before a retort could rise from my breast, Sheriff led the way out of the room and through the clinic. 'Don't go starting a fight,' he murmured to me, a hand on my elbow. 'You may not be sticking around much longer, but your Uncle Bert will be, and I doubt the Councilwoman is happy with him anymore. I'll look out for him, but don't go causing more trouble for the poor man.'

I sighed but nodded. Sheriff was absolutely right at the time, and I accepted that. Besides, meaningfully or not, Diana had given me consent to finish my research. I had plenty of notes to refer to, both written and mental, though the madman's words circled my mind like vultures above a carcass.

'Oh, and one more thing,' Sheriff grumbled. 'Don't go down into that mine again, else I will have to deal with you. Right now, I've got too much on my plate with this awful revelation—' he gestured back toward the consultation room with his thumb '—so we'll keep it our little secret. Don't mess with me, though, Mr. Wolfe.'

'Of course, Sheriff,' I replied, conscious of the nervous hitch in my voice. 'I've got all I need now, anyway. A few days, and I'll be gone.'

He nodded, and only now released his admittedly gentle grip on my arm. Outside the clinic, he offered to give me a ride, but the weather was reasonably cool, so I politely declined and walked back to Uncle Bert's house.

I couldn't stop thinking about the madman's insane confession. That something lurked in that pit of bones sounded absolutely insane, yet the very fact that man had somehow survived into his hundreds despite the evident emaciation that consumed him suggested that unusual forces were indeed at work in Manhattan.

A shiver coursed through me, and I looked back up at the eerie, green-tinted sky.

CHAPTER 10
A SLAVE TO THE PEN

Bert was astonished when I told him about the mad cadaver interred in the cell. I'm not sure what he'd imagined when Diana revealed a miner was still alive, but the way he sank back in his chair, eyes wide and mouth agape, told me that it hadn't touched on the reality. How could it? No one that old should have been able to survive such crippling emaciation, yet I had witnessed a strange strength in his creaking bones.

Recalling the awful interview was enough to make my throat close up. He had paced around that dustless dungeon as though he possessed the vigor of a youth, though his skeletal frame suggested otherwise. Was there some truth to his claims that "something older than time" was keeping him alive?

It sounded preposterous, yet I could not find a logical explanation for his longevity. My head ached, and I pinched the bridge of my nose to chase it away. No luck.

'It's all very strange,' Bert muttered, tapping the arm of his chair. 'What are you going to do now? Head back into the mine?'

The suggestion made my chest go tight, and I found myself glaring at my unkempt uncle. 'Go back?' I scoffed. 'I don't think so; Sheriff's already warned me that if I keep digging around in there he'll come after me—not to mention the Councilwoman's going to be gunning for you—and I'd rather not make myself public enemy number one. Besides, I'm not sure if there's anything else worth finding down there.' Bert nodded along, though appeared disappointed by my decision, unable to understand my hesitation. 'It's not worth trying to dig anything out. The place is dangerous, whether it is some kind of gas, or if that lunatic was actually on to something… and after what I saw in there… no, I'm not going back.'

'Well…' Bert hesitated, and then shook his head, whatever protestation he had in mind dying on the spot. 'I guess you'll be leaving, then.'

'Not yet,' I replied, forcing a smile. 'I'm going to stick around for a few more days, just to organize my notes.'

Maybe I should have left. I had plenty of information, and it wasn't like my book was going to be about Manhattan alone, yet I felt compelled to remain. *Just in case I need more information*, I told myself.

Bert smiled at me, though that smile did not extend to his eyes. 'Right. Good. A few more days.'

***

Together, Bert and I cleared a space in his attic for me to use as a makeshift office. There was an old desk buried amidst the dust and cobwebbed old furniture that we cleaned up, and Bert was able to dig out a reasonably intact chair. We placed both near the boarded-up attic window, and after some debate I convinced my uncle to remove one of the wooden planks to admit some light.

Admittedly, doing so also let in a breeze; hot air surrounded me as I worked during the day, whilst the icy air of the midnight desert stole the house's heat at night. Uncle Albert even went so far as to retrieve some blankets from his cellar, not without some grumbling.

I remained in Manhattan for another three days, spending most of my time secluded in the attic, surrounded by scraps of paper. I had done a fair job of keeping track of my notes, and my proficient memory had retained what was not yet written down. Every bit of information I had on the mystery of Manhattan Mine was soon piled up before me.

Over those three days, however, an atmosphere of dread weighed down upon the old, forgotten town. I lost count of the number of times I gazed out through the gap in the window, eyes lingering on the decrepit buildings, all painted by a hint of green.

Every time I noticed that eerie color that seemed to stain the air, my head ached as though it was being squeezed. On a few occasions, when I closed my eyes to chase away the pain, an image of skulls assembled around the cursed cave assaulted my vision.

These same images tormented me in my sleep, stirring me to wakefulness with frustrating regularity. My eyes stung almost every day, the hot air outside worsening their dryness, and I could feel the throbbing effects of exhaustion in every inch of my being. A glance in one of Uncle Bert's clouded mirrors showed the greying of the skin around my eyes.

Bert was much the same, muttering to me every morning that he hadn't slept, and kept looking out his window, watching the ridge. 'There's never anything up there,' he said, downing his coffee. 'Nothing moves, nothing changes, but I just keep looking.'

On the third day, with my initial notes complete, I was about to start piecing together the chronological narrative of Manhattan Mine. As I scribbled down the first entry in my timeline—*1883: Mine opened*—my uncle suddenly burst into the room, dark-eyed and trembling.

'Strange things are happening, Maxwell,' he slurred, shuffling over to stand beside me. His bloodshot eyes scanned the documents upon the desk. 'Strange things, I tell you. The Barker boy came round half an hour ago, bringing me my goods, and he had some news to share. Strange news. Frightful news. Are you listening, boy?'

I nodded, afraid to interrupt. He was particularly worked up about something, and far fierier than he had been even when the Councilwoman came to visit.

'You remember how I told you we never get coyotes around here? Hell, we never get any animals that I can remember seeing. Well, all of a sudden everyone's scared to leave their homes 'cause we've got rabid, mangy dogs the size of horses wandering about at night. You're always up here, looking out that window; have you seen them?'

I hadn't, but he didn't wait for a response before rambling on. 'I haven't seen them myself, but I don't like looking outside anyway. Especially not the last few nights. The moon just doesn't look right anymore. Have you noticed that it seems to be a full moon every night? That's just not right. You know what else isn't right? The water just doesn't taste as it did. I tell you, something's just wrong lately, and it all started when you came out of that mine.'

Breathless, he placed a hand on my shoulder, brow furrowing. 'Say, you feeling okay? You look like death warmed over.'

I debated whether or not to tell him about the intermittent headaches and sleepless nights. No doubt he had surmised the latter himself; what I knew I shouldn't mention were the dark conclusions I was beginning to come to.

About how the mine seemed to be alive in some way, or was at least an extension of something living. My nightmares reflected those experienced by the townsfolk—at least according to Sheriff's retelling—and I was beginning to conclude that the madman may have been telling more truths than I initially believed.

The mine was holding people in Manhattan; what had been a subtle pull before was now a nightmarish claw in their minds. Somehow, despite my short time here, it was gripping me, too.

I never should have entered that mine.

Facing my uncle, and forcing a smile, I simply said, 'I've just had a few rough nights, that's all.' I gestured to all my notes. 'I guess I'm just getting a bit too involved in my work.'

He nodded, then shrugged. 'Well, just keep an eye out, okay? And let me know if anything weird happens. Something's not right. Something's really not right.'

Patting me on the shoulder, Bert turned and left the room, disappearing amidst the creaking of worn, wooden stairs.

Alone, I shivered, and was grateful I hadn't left the house since my visit to the clinic.

If there were now giant dogs lurking in Manhattan's shadows, then this town was quickly becoming unsafe. Another day of notes and I'd leave, before the mine held me here forever.

***

Another two days passed, and I was a quarter of the way through a rough draft of a chapter dedicated to Manhattan Mine. Three different versions of the timeline were spread out across the table, none of which I was entirely satisfied with. I couldn't place why, but they all felt inaccurate and incomplete, despite the copious amounts of documentation I had inspected.

My self-imposed solitude, too, was beginning to wear on my mind. Perhaps it was simply a lack of sleep, but I was beginning to feel as though a rope was tethering me to the desk. How was I meant to leave the town if I couldn't even step away from my writing?

It was as I was pondering this that Bert entered the attic, though in a far more reserved manner than the other day. His hands trembled much as they had before, a product of his exhaustion, but his voice was level.

'The Barker boy... he's disappeared,' he said, the hint of a sob catching in his throat. 'His mother came by an hour ago; he didn't make it home from his deliveries. They searched all of yesterday. He seemed well when he came by, and I told her as much, and told her he would be headed straight home.

'I fear for him, Max. He was calm as the desert when he told me about those awful dogs. Such a frightful prospect, yet his childish bravado rendered him unafraid. I wish he had been afraid, Max. Maybe then he'd be home and safe.

'I'm in no shape to head out and aid in the search, but would you go in my stead? A Wolfe should help, after all; the boy's been such a help to me, and I don't want to see his family left not knowing what's happened to him.'

Given strength by Bert's heartbroken tone, I rose from my seat, legs aching, reminding me just how long I'd been sitting without moving. 'Of course,' I said, squeezing his arm.

CHAPTER 11
THE SEARCH MUST GO ON

A small force was out in search of little Johnny Barker, moving in bands of four to six people, each taking a different corner of the town. When first I left Uncle Bert's house, I searched alone, but within twenty minutes of walking around Manhattan, assaulted by the oppressive heat of the green-tinted sun, I had found myself assimilated by one of the search parties.

Most of the faces around me were unrecognizable, but there was one who I knew: Martha. She, like the others, wore a face overwhelmed by exhaustion and concern, dark bags circling her bloodshot eyes.

Stepping in beside her, I asked, 'How long have you been searching?'

She shrugged, her eyes constantly drifting across the road ahead of us, or into the passages between buildings. Everywhere we looked, there just seemed to be more sand, or the occasional tumbleweed. 'I came out to look as soon as Mrs. Barker brought the news,' she replied. I noted how her voice had lost its intensity, becoming little more than a whisper. 'I can't just sit back and do nothing whilst a little boy is lost. Mr. Barker has always been a fine patron at the bar, and Johnny has been a helpful hand for so many people around here...' She shook her head and sighed. 'How could the boy just disappear?'

I swallowed. 'Bert... he told me that there had been some... sightings around town.'

'Of the boy?' Martha said, hope flickering into her eyes. I shook my head, and that spark was extinguished. 'Oh... you mean the dogs, or whatever the hell they are.' I nodded. 'Have you not left the house the past few days? No? Well, that's why we're all wandering around in these here little search parties, and probably why everyone's quite so concerned that the kid has disappeared. You see, it's not just *sightings* anymore.'

'What do you mean?' I inquired. Something in her tone set ice creeping down my spine, warning of dark news ahead.

'As I said, it's not just been sightings. There have been *attacks*, Mr. Wolfe, and not just a quick bite and then the beast runs away,' Martha explained, fidgeting with her hands, squeezing her fingers. 'We started the searches on our own the other day. No groups, just concerned folk going for a wander to see if they could find little Johnny. We wondered whether he'd fallen into a hole somewhere or had tripped on the walk home and broken his leg; something like that. Then Jonah Clark didn't come home.

'Sheriff found him this morning, all torn up. Guts everywhere, he said, like an animal got 'im.

That wasn't all, though. I wish it was—and it's why we're looking everywhere again. Last night there was other attacks, too. No one dead, thank the Lord, but people are hurt. It was those dogs... no, I don't think they are dogs, actually. Dogs don't look like that.'

I had not been keeping an eye out for Johnny at all this whole time, too caught up in what Martha was saying. Things seemed to be getting worse, and I was becoming increasingly aware of my desire to leave. I *needed* to leave; so why hadn't I?

'You saw one?' My question prompted Martha to glare at me as though I were accusing her of lying. I most certainly wasn't.

'Oh, I saw one alright,' she said, voice trembling. Her already washed-out face turned deathly pale. 'One came to my bar last night, scratching at my door, my windows, my wall. It circled the entire place, like it was looking for a way in, sniffing at every crack. The ground seemed to rupture under its feet, and all I could smell was... was *rot*. I know what rot smells like; too many of the folk around here leave food on the floor in my bar, and sometimes I don't notice it until the rot sets in.' She shuddered. 'Oh, but that thing smelled so much worse. And its eyes; God preserve me, its eyes were dark and sunken things, almost as if they were too small for its skull.

'It was skinny, Mr. Wolfe. Too skinny, like it had starved to death long ago but was somehow still walking. Horrible, hairless thing, too, except for this line of thick hairs—well, I guess they were more like spikes—running down its back. Tell me, what is dog skin meant to look like under all that fur? Is it meant to look like grey scales? Because that's what this thing had, and it didn't look right. It didn't look right at all.'

She breathed fast and had to pause to catch her breath. The search party halted around us. One of them asked if Martha was okay and suggested she might want to go back to the bar.

'No, no, I'm fine,' Martha replied. 'We've got to find the boy. I couldn't live with myself if he's been got by one of those beasts.'

Slowly, the small band of searchers continued on their route. Every so often, someone called for Johnny Barker, but still there was no sign.

'A couple of the townsfolk are in the clinic now, you know. They saw one of those dog-things and tried to chase it off their property. The thing snapped their legs clean off...' Martha shook her head. 'We've got to find him...'

All I could do was nod. Words failed me, my eyes turning toward the ridge, toward the mine. If only I hadn't gone in there. I couldn't help but feel I was somehow to blame for this mess.

***

We had no luck in our search that day. Returning home, I found Bert sat at his clouded window, staring out even though he surely couldn't see anything.

'Bert,' I said, grabbing his attention. 'I need to leave. I've got enough for my book—for a chapter or two, anyway—and things are getting a bit too crazy around here. I'm sorry.'

He didn't turn to me, just kept gazing at the dust-caked glass. 'We need to find the boy, Maxwell. Help them find the boy first, then you can go. Please.'

I approached him, placing a hand on his shoulder. 'Uncle, really, I don't feel like it's safe—'

'Find the Barker boy, Maxwell. For me. Please...' he turned to face me, his movements stiff. 'Please.'

His eyes were bloodshot, red-rimmed and wet. Genuine pain made them dull, and my heart broke for him. Kneeling down beside my decrepit uncle, I clasped his hands in mine and nodded. 'Okay. Okay, I'll find him.'

What a foolish promise that was.

***

The searches continued for three more days, our numbers reducing with each passing night. There were more attacks, I was told, so less of the townsfolk dared to leave their homes. People stopped hearing from one another. The last church congregation had consisted of barely a dozen souls. On the second day Martha did not show up, and by the third only myself and one other, a young man named Frankie Farrell, had dared to patrol our assigned corner of Manhattan.

Halfway through the search he broke down in tears, gibbered an apology, then ran home, leaving me alone. I cursed Frankie for abandoning me but continued my search. As far as I was aware, there hadn't been any attacks by the beasts during daylight, and so felt somewhat confident in my own safety.

'Johnny! It's Max Wolfe, Albert's nephew!' I called, over and over again, until my throat was raw. My feet soon started aching, shoes wearing away, as I plodded along my patrol. Eventually evening approached, and deciding I was unlikely to find any sign of little Johnny Barker along the same route we had walked for the past few days, I altered my course.

Still I called for him, my eyes investigating every object of interest in hopes of finding some trace of his presence.

Soon enough, I realized I was walking along the route towards the clinic. A part of me wanted to visit the men who had been so viciously attacked by the strange mutant hounds—if they still lived—but I knew that doing so would not lead me to Johnny.

It was as I was thinking this, however, that I spotted something that set my heart aflutter like a bird that did not wish to be caged.

Upon the road I noticed a trail of blood, dark blots seeping into the sandy ground, quickly turning black. Concern drove me to follow the trail, off to the left of the road, into a narrow passage between two houses. Not quite an alleyway, but similarly shadowed. There, upon the ground ahead, was what appeared to be a bag of trash.

Approaching, I was assailed by a stench of iron and shit; covering my mouth with my arm, I hardly dared approach, my mind suggesting awful possibilities. Still I crept forward. I had to know what I was seeing.

It was, as I feared, a corpse, bloody and torn. Yet it did not appear to be the victim of an animal attack. Though the cuts were extensive, clearly frenzied, they appeared clean, as though produced by a blade of some kind. Blood still seeped from the gashes.

Crouching closer, I was certain this wasn't little Johnny Barker. The body was far too large, though the damage made it impossible to know exactly who it could be. Clothes had been reduced to rags, encrusted in so much gore they only existed in varying degrees of red. I almost reached out to touch it, but held myself back; what would that accomplish? Why would I want to touch it?

Then I noticed the body had *no head*. I gasped, trembling, struggling not to vomit, frozen to the spot. What had happened here?

I backed away, rising, eyes returning to the trail of drying, thickening blood. Leaving the passage, the stench of the cadaver still fresh in my nose, I shuffled back out onto the road. The shock had rendered me numb; I knew I should have been crying, or calling for help, but instead I simply stood, dumbstruck, in the beating sun.

Hands shaking, I turned to follow the trail, kicking up the sand around my feet. It billowed around me, stinging my eyes, but I did not lose sight of the trail. It led me a considerable distance down the road, alternating between thick pools and tiny spots, and I could not help but wonder just how much blood that poor soul had lost before succumbing to their wounds.

And what had happened to their head?

The trail terminated—or rather, began—before me, and my chest tightened so that I stumbled, gasping for air. I should have predicted it as soon as I saw the blood.

It was coming from the clinic.

CHAPTER 12
MADNESS REIGNS

It took barely a moment for concern to overcome my alarm, sending me sprinting towards the building. The blood grew thicker, the pools larger, and when I reached the door my entire body seized, gripped by shock at the horror that greeted me.

Not a single floorboard appeared free of blood, which pooled sticky and malodorous all around. The doctor's desk had been utterly destroyed, reduced to a million splinters. A small metal handle amongst the debris told me what it had once been, but even worse was the torn up, red-stained mass that rested within the chaos.

Only the white coat offered any chance of identification. That poor young doctor, who had run the clinic singlehandedly with, I assumed, little-to-no formal training, had been violently eviscerated. At a glance, it seemed that her body had been used as a club; whatever killed her slammed her down on the desk, obliterating it.

Beyond this unfortunate corpse was another, piled unceremoniously on the floor beside a steel bed, similarly unrecognizable. Most upsetting of all was that it, like the poor, pursued corpse in the alley, had no head. Much of the blood that painted the floor must have originated from this brutal decapitation.

I say brutal, for there were unmistakable signs of tearing all around the neck. The head had been wrenched from the body.

Somehow, I succeeded in not vomiting, though I was entirely frozen in that doorway for more time than I care to think about. Perhaps there was something inside me that had seen this coming; that had predicted this gruesome outcome of my foolish foray into Manhattan Mine. It is the only reason I can think of for me not going immediately mad.

Rather, as I regained faculty over my limbs, I turned toward the door marked "Consultations", where I had so recently accompanied Diana and Sheriff as we faced the impossible prisoner below. To my utter horror, the door had been shattered from within, barely upon its hinges.

The truth of what had happened here began to sink in, but I also had to be sure. Overcoming my revulsion at the gory spectacle that had greeted me, I gingerly proceeded toward the room.

Within, I found that this door was not the only one to have been broken. The section of wall that hid the secret staircase into that inhumane dungeon had been torn away; it now lay shattered upon the wall opposite, a single shard somehow piercing the window itself. The stench of damp and rot from below had spread to this room, but I pushed through the foul sensation and peered down the stairs.

Nothing moved. Nothing made a sound.

Cautiously, I proceeded down into the dingy domain, but did not remain there long. The iron bars of the cell had been twisted, forced aside, *and the mummy-like madman was gone*. I scrambled away, back into the clinic proper, and stumbled my way back to the door. Passing the desk, my eyes fell upon the doctor again, and I cried out when it dawned on me that her head, too, had been stolen.

Frightened, desperate thoughts fought in my mind. I had to get help; I had to get away; I had to tell Uncle Bert. Finally, I landed on a decision I hoped was the right one: tell Sheriff.

***

Sprinting along the sandy streets of Manhattan like a heat-addled maniac—and truthfully feeling the effects of the pounding sun even as it descended over the horizon—I struggled to find my way to Sheriff. Thus far I had not had reason to visit his home nor his office. In the end, it transpired that these places were one and the same.

The door had been locked tight, no doubt in the interests of warding off the dog-things that I had been lucky enough not to encounter. That the lawman of the town, however, appeared to have sealed himself inside was somehow even more frightening that anything else I had discovered. A gruesome murder was one thing, but a Sheriff unwilling to protect the people... I shudder to think of the implications.

Sweat-soaked, I hammered on the door, keeping up my percussive demands until the latch clicked and Sheriff, dark-eyed, pale, and slumping at the shoulders, unlatched it and eased it open. He, like Uncle Bert upon our first meeting, did not open it fully. His haunted eyes met mine, and with a voice like wheezing he hissed, 'Get outta here. Get. I don't want to hear nothing of you.'

Ignoring his cold greeting, I blurted, 'There's been a killing! Everyone at the clinic is dead, and that madman in the basement is gone! Blood everywhere, Sheriff, and their heads; their heads are gone!'

'Shut your mouth,' Sheriff snapped, though it was a mercy he did not immediately slam the door in my face. 'You're as mad as everyone else in this godforsaken town. There's something in the air, you know. I can smell it. See it. Something in the air, and it's makin' everyone sick. Including you. Coming here and screaming about beheadings and madmen. You get outta this place, y'hear me? Take that car of yours and leave before you get too sick. I ain't leaving my house. It'll make me sick too. Go on, go!'

Then he did slam the door, but at that point I was already turning to run. To seek help elsewhere. If Sheriff was no use, then I would go to the townsfolk. Perhaps manmade murder as opposed to the killings committed by uncanny animals would stir them to action, though as I dashed along the roads, I wondered whether "manmade" was truly the right word.

Was the madman not possessed of a strength his body should have lacked? Did he not claim to be empowered by something older than time? My mind ached and my stomach lurched as I entertained the insane idea that we may have been facing a far more macabre power than could be believed. And what chance did man have against something so ancient?

Finally, I approached Martha's and surged inside. Unlike Sheriff's, it was unlocked, though I was to find no help here. The entire establishment was empty, except for Martha, slumped over the bar, muttering to herself. Hoping she could at least point me towards the other souls of this tortured town, I approached her, placing a hand on her shoulder.

Before I could utter a word, she turned, eyes red and teary. 'Oh, a newcomer!' she exclaimed. 'Always good to see a fresh face around Manhattan. Here, let me fix you a drink. Just give me...' She attempted to stand from the seat, then staggered and sat down again. 'Say, have you met my ma? She knows all the secrets around this town; used to sneak around as a child, didn't you, ma?' Her face turned towards the seat beside her, and I followed her gaze.

No one there, yet she continued to speak, not to me but to the unseen companion. Her long-deceased mother, if her speech was to be believed. Much of what she said was gibberish, but then she said something that made my blood run cold.

'Tell him what you were just telling me, ma. Yeah, about the man at the mine, the one with a cloak of blood. He's going to make us rich, right? Yeah, he's gonna get all the gold out, and we're gonna be saved.'

I shook my head, cried out in despair, and again rushed into the thoroughfares of Manhattan town. Would everyone else be just as mad as Martha had become? Would any of them even open their doors to me? Insanity seemed certain, for had Frankie

Farrell not been at the edge of madness when he abandoned the search?

Half-mad myself, it seemed, from hopelessness and heatstroke, I realized that Manhattan was lost. Whatever power emanated from the mouth of the mine, staining the sky green and melting everyone's minds, had blanketed the entire community. For what purpose I could not fathom, but I knew I must escape.

Hurrying back to Uncle Bert's home, I charged inside, not caring about the creaking of the hinges or the integrity of the door. My eyes, first, glanced upstairs, towards the attic where my desk and notes waited, but they seemed so frightfully insignificant now. The information remained inside my mind; no, I was there for something far more tangible. Striding into the lounge, I found my old uncle slumped in his chair, knuckles turned white as he gripped the arms. His eyes glowed with mania, but I crouched down in front of him nonetheless, reaching out, shaking him.

'Get up, Uncle Bert,' I urged. 'Get up, we're leaving this town. Leaving it all behind. Get up, get in my car. I'll take you far away from all this misery and madness, I promise. Get up.'

Bert simply shook his head at me. 'No, no, Maxwell, we have to stay here. Grandpa Otto won't be long. We can't leave without him; he's bringing us some gold from the mine... going to make us rich.'

I tried to pull him up from his seat, but he slapped at me with his gnarled hands, nails scratching my skin. 'No! We have to wait for Grandpa Otto!' he snapped, and there was something in his tone, dark and unpleasant, that suggested he was willing to cause further harm to get his own way. Pleading would not change his mind.

Apologizing for the abandonment I was about to impose on him—just as his own brother had years ago—I stood up and strode from the house, towards my car.

Only a short drive stood between me and escape. Forcing myself to abandon my notes and my uncle, I jumped into my car and set the keys to the ignition. It was time to go, I told myself. It was time to go... yet I could not bring myself to start the engine.

Martha's words clung to my mind like a hook in a fish. *"The man at the mine, the one with a cloak of blood"*. My eyes turned toward that dreadful ridge, neck aching as I faced the rocky cliffs, within which that cursed cave with its abhorrent altar had been discovered.

Crying out for the third time that day, I abandoned the vehicle, keys still inside, and returned to Uncle Bert's house. He continued to ramble about great-grandpa Otto whilst I retrieved that long-dead ancestor's gear from around the house, dressing myself as I did that fateful day when I so daftly delved into Manhattan Mine.

My uncle's eyes fell upon me, and his face split into a smile. 'Grandpa Otto! I told Max you'd be back soon. Did you bring the gold? We can't leave without the gold.'

I just shook my head, not knowing what to say; any words would either destroy the illusion, risking further damage to his psyche, or reveal me as an imposter. The latter, I feared, may have resulted in violence.

Without offering Uncle Bert any further acknowledgement, I hefted the pickaxe over my shoulder and left the house, heading out into the back garden. I began the trek up that rocky ridge, dreading the madness in Manhattan Mine.

CHAPTER 13
ALL THAT GLITTERS IS NOT GOD

My body revolted against my efforts to enter the black maw of the mine, fearing the confines of those tunnels, and memories of the terrible presence within. That the madman from beneath the clinic was here—or had at least been here recently—was definite; spatters of blood had led me up to the entrance, almost inviting me. The unhinged sectors of my mind suggested that he was leading the way, in case I had forgotten.

A damp, putrid scent lingered at the mine's mouth. It was cloying and choking, enough to make me gag. Yet again I experienced the urge to turn away, climb in my car, and abandon Manhattan to its decay. Only, I knew that as I sat in the driver's seat my eyes would again be drawn to this spot, and I would be compelled to make the climb again.

That would be my cycle, until I keeled over from exhaustion or the mad murderer returned and took my head too. No... I knew that I had to face him. I had come here seeking information, uncovering a mystery, and now there were only a few more pieces of the puzzle to find.

If I could discover the full story, I told myself, maybe I could save the sanity of the poor souls of Manhattan.

It was that conclusion that encouraged me to push through the awful air and enter the mine again. Uncle Bert's powerful flashlight illuminated the muddy mineshafts, but it was not the light that I followed. Upon entering that subterranean nightmare, a force led the way. I realized, then, that I had neglected to secure myself with a rope this time; instead, hands were pulling upon a tether that led me deeper, and deeper, and deeper.

My body remembered the way to that terrible, natural-yet-outlandish cave; perhaps those tugging sensations were my body trying to pull me *away* from my chosen path. It is impossible to know.

Signs of my quarry lay at my feet. As above, so below: the spatters of blood, no doubt from the sundered skulls or—if Martha was to be believed— a cloak of flesh, continued here.

The hot air of the higher passages gave way to that ominous chill; then the smooth walls of artificial excavation were replaced by the jagged rockery of primeval caverns. Again, the stench struck me, yet it was terror that made my gut cramp. I stumbled, resting against the walls.

By then I had come close enough to the evil glow of that frightening final hollow, and could see the stacked corpses of fetid fauna. There were, without a doubt, more there now, including great horse-sized beasts with grey, flaking skin, spiked spines, and great mastiff jaws laden with razor teeth.

These were the great mangy hounds that had been seen during the mad Manhattan nights, when the moon was made green by the mists of the mine. Why, though, were they now dead? I had forced myself to delve back into the darkness, promising myself I would uncover the final secrets, yet I was faced now with new questions.

Was there any end to the mysteries? I had no way of knowing unless I entered the dark heart of Manhattan.

Stepping over and around this mound of bloated, stinking corpses, I made my entrance into the cursed central chamber, pickaxe at the ready. Upon laying eyes on the scene, however, I froze again, ready to fall to my knees in a gibbering wreck if I could not, for a few more seconds, hold myself together.

It was truly a sight from the depths of hell, beyond the imaginings of Milton or Dante. All that was missing was the flames themselves! All upon the rock was painted, in drying blood, ornate occultic symbols that made my skin itch and writhed in my mind. The lichen-like substance that grew there appeared brighter, as though fed by the sacred fluid spattered around them. Tattered skins hung from hooks in the roof, dripping ruby-like droplets upon the floor, which shattered and flowed to that grotesque grey stone at the center. A corpse, stripped of its skin, had been impaled upon the stalactites above, held there I knew not how; beneath it, curled in a ball, shivering, crying, was a small boy.

Young Johnny Barker. He had set eyes on things he should never have seen.

The poor child…

Between he and I stood the madman, still skeletal and withered, yet now stripped naked except for a coat of wet, still-pink flesh he had draped about his shoulders. Whether he heard my footsteps, my gasp, or simply *sensed me* as I entered, I do not know; whatever gave me away, he turned, the skin sickeningly slapping upon itself. His grin, which creased his rough, dry skin, threatening to tear it, was somehow worse than all that had come before.

'I knew you'd come,' he rasped. 'Oh, I'm so glad you came. Are you ready to play your part? You reawakened the god of bones, after all. Ah, but where is your cloak? Did you not bring your own raiment to this ritual? Well, you shan't be sharing mine, and the boy's skin is much too small for you. Well, you shall have to go without. Still, I will permit you to be the one to end the child. Cut his throat so the god of bones can emerge.'

As he turned further to meet my glare, I noticed something in his hands that, were I not already frightened to the edge of stability by the butchery before me, would surely have sent me scurrying from that cave. It was the head of Dr. Wilson, eyes wide, mouth agape, silenced in the moment of her final, terrible scream.

'Come, come,' the madman went on. 'You even brought a weapon. Crude, perhaps—I much prefer the intimacy of the knife—but it will do. Come, come, crush the boy's body. Give his blood and head to the lord of bones.'

His insidious invitation stirred me to action. Strength returned to my muscles, and I gripped the haft of my weapon tighter. 'I will not play a part in this insanity. Let the boy go, and then let us be done with this.'

The madman blinked at me, the sinister smile giving way to a glimmer of confusion. It did not last long, though, and then he laughed—the laugh set ice into my veins, and I shuddered, fearing that I was about to lose grip on both the pickaxe and my mind.

'What has been started cannot be stopped,' he cried. 'They tried before; they tried to blast the mine shut, but the tunnels stayed open. The god of bones took their explosives and swallowed them whole, and they ran like the rats they are. But then no one came to the mine anymore, and the god of bones was not yet satisfied, so he had to remain here, buried, waiting.

'But then you—oh you wonderful meddler—you came, and you met his eyes and he knew it was time to try again. The hounds have brought so many to him, plucked from their homes without anyone's knowledge. They have given their blood and bodies to him. Come, come, look at the pit now. It's almost full. Two more skulls and the god of bones can be reborn, and all the world will tremble at his might!'

As he spoke, I noticed that the unbelonging stone seemed to have shifted aside, revealing that pit in its entirety. It was, however, a deep, black pit no longer; it was full of skulls, far more and far fresher than those I had seen before. Hair and flesh still clung to the white surface. Had so many of Manhattan's residents truly been killed? Was that, I considered, shocked at the thought, why there had been fewer and fewer searchers each day?

Confusion, anger, and fear surged within me.

With a wordless cry, I started forward and swung the pickaxe at his head. Again, his body moved as it should not, and he ducked under the strike with fantastic flexibility. The counterstrike came not from a knife but from the head of the butchered Doctor Wilson; her frightful stare came at my face, her teeth tearing my cheek as I took the blow.

Ignoring the warmth that streamed down my face, but stumbling all the same, I whirled the pickaxe again, hitting nothing. Beyond our combatting forms, little Johnny screamed, his wails twisted by the coiling tunnels of Manhattan Mine.

The madman took horrendous glee in the melee. Maniacal laughs accompanied every attempted attack with his odious weapon; the blood from his cloak of flayed flesh spattered everything, staining great-grandpa Otto's overalls, mingling with the redness that flowed from my wound.

After a myriad of missed swipes, I landed a strike, the sharp edge of the pickaxe sinking into a bony, protruding shoulder. My opponent yelped, growled; he dropped the head, which rolled away from us and toward the sacrilegious stone.

As I delivered a kick to the madman, recovering my weapon and sending him staggering away, I watched as the head fell upon the other bones, becoming a fixture of that ghastly pit. As if in response, a tremble coursed through the rocks around us.

Despite his wound, the madman raised both arms, triumphant. 'Do you hear it? The god of bones stirs. One more head in the pit and it will be done!'

Taking full advantage of his distraction, I charged at him, slamming his unnatural body into the rocks. He stumbled away, fell to his knees, and before he could recover I brought my weapon down into his skull. Bone cracked, blood spurted, and a wet, gurgling rattle emerged from his throat.

I could not bring myself to pull the mining tool free—and perhaps feared that to do so would somehow allow the madman to stand up again—so turned away from the thing I had killed and knelt in front of little Johnny Barker. It took all my willpower not to look at the pit of bones and the battered, staring head of the ill-fated doctor.

'Hey, Johnny, right?' I said to him. He sobbed, but nodded, body trembling. 'I'm going to get you out of here, okay? Just take my hand and follow me.' He did as I said, tentatively climbing down from the blood-spattered rock. 'Good, good. Close your eyes and let me lead the—'

I was cut off by another shaking off the earth, this time seeming to possess a nameless, ethereal anger. Now my eyes did turn to the pit of bones, as I recalled the mad miner's blatherings about a god and ancient entities. The pit was nearly filled; what if the power that supposedly predated time itself had decided that this was enough bones after all?

My hand quivered like the rock above and around us, even as it held that of Johnny Barker. There was no way he didn't feel it; his sobs started again, and he froze on the spot. To his credit, he did keep his eyes squeezed shut. As such, he didn't have time to see what happened next, and I pray he was oblivious to the outcome.

As the trembling continued, the ceiling of the cave cracked, loose rocks tumbling down around us. The hooks dropped down, skin slapping on stone as it landed, even more blood being flung around the eerie, crimson-colored chamber; above us, the stalactites shuddered.

I saw it coming, but fear froze me. As one does when witnessing a car crash, all I could do was watch as the column of prehistoric rock dropped. Johnny was crushed; warm, wet jewels splashed upon my astonished face.

Horrifically, his head survived, eyes still squeezed shut, mouth downturned. It teetered on the spot for a moment, then spun, toppled, and began a dreadful bowling motion toward the pit.

My limbs were too slow to reanimate. By the time I could move again, Johnny's head had landed upon the pile of bones. It looked as though he were simply buried within them, with his head above the surface, yet the crimson liquid that spread over the surrounding bones made it clear this was not the case.

I screamed then, I admit. It was a scream of misery and shock, intertwined with a most terrible grief. How could I have come so close to saving the boy, only to have his life taken before my very eyes? Tears streamed through the blood on my cheeks.

The madness was not to end here, however. By God, I wish it had.

CHAPTER 14
THANK YOU, MANHATTAN, AND GOODNIGHT

Beneath Johnny Barker's head, the profane pit shifted. At first, its dreadful contents sunk by a couple of inches; a tiny, hopeful thought suggested that it was merely a consequence of the tremors that wracked the mine. However, an instant later and the bones continued to descend, surging over one another like liquid, though the grinding and clacking of skulls upon femurs—and all other manner of skeletal pieces—proved they remained very much intact.

Was there, then, indeed a god of bones waiting down there? Had it finally been granted the final head necessary for its unholy emergence?

The fear my body had displayed when I had first sought to re-enter Manhattan Mine swelled within me again, seeking to drag me away from the dreadful occurrence though I doubted the surface would be any safer. I almost allowed it to, muscles ready to take flight, abandoning flashlight and pickaxe alike and praying I would find my way to freedom.

As I was turning to the one option of escape, however, the words of the madman echoed in my mind. Particularly, I recalled that, as he put it, *"the god of bones took their explosives and swallowed them whole"*. If this pit of retreating remains was connected to this supposed deity, then did it not make sense that this was where those explosives had ended up?

Reaching into the pocket of great-grandpa Otto's overalls, I retrieved the stick of dynamite that had so fortunately been secreted in the chest. It had, somehow, not been damaged in my fight with the insane, century-old architect of so many murders.

Smashing Uncle Bert's flashlight, I was plunged into darkness; only the green lichen on the rocks offered any luminescence, and that sickly glow increased my fear a thousandfold, even as the ground continued to shake around me. Fiddling with the electronics, I was able to ignite a spark, which caught the lengthy fuse of the dynamite.

It began to fizzle in my hand, and I mustered all my courage as I crawled to the pit. The bones continued to fall away from me, into the darkness, revealing again the sparkling of the precious stones in the rock at its edges. Far below, I could feel living eyes upon me, as opposed to the extinct glares of the skulls before. A fear of things beyond my understanding, and beyond what should exist, clawed at my mind, sending shivers through my body, threatening to lock every limb in place.

But then I released the stick of dynamite into that hole.

Before it was even out of my sight, I found the strength to clamber to my feet and retreated from that hellish place. My feet carried me up and through the darkness, though I regularly collided with the walls, scraping holes into the overalls that had for so long been preserved by the antique case. I do not know how I found my way back out, but upon emerging onto a hill bathed in jade moonlight I did not stop to wonder.

The earthquake I had experienced within the malevolent Manhattan Mine continued out here, and as I rushed back down the rock-strewn road, I could see the historied buildings of the town crumbling. The sign atop Martha's bar had fallen free of its spot above the door; the church spire had collapsed down into itself, shattering the building entirely. Where the town hall had been was now only a ruin of flaking timber.

With more sorrow than expected, I wondered whether Diana and the other, unseen, councilor had been inside at the time.

There was, though, no time to find out. Behind me, there came a great upheaval of the earth, and the ground beneath my feet cracked and crumbled. Boulders bombarded the old forsaken road to the mine, and I can scarcely believe that I somehow avoided them.

Reaching Uncle Bert's house, I found it had succumbed to the terrible tremors, now roofless, the walls caved in and blocking all entry. Even if I could have reached him, though, I doubted my unfortunate uncle would have come away with me; his mind was lost, just like the town that had sapped his life away.

Instead, I leapt into my car, slammed shut the door, and brought its engine to life. It was a relief when the first turn of the key produced a roar of successful ignition. Putting the car to motion, I accelerated onto the road and drove as directly as possible away from the mine and towards the faint roads that had led me here in the first place.

Behind me, the ground continued to move and split, seeming to elevate itself, as though something moved beneath it, fighting to punch through the ground and emerge onto the surface. The more it fought, the more the earth was rearranged. All the buildings of Manhattan crumbled to dust behind me, the lives of all the frightened, maddened residents crushed within just as poor Johnny Baker had been.

What few inhabitants remained outside were swallowed by the ground. Some saw me pass, screaming, waving their arms at me, but I knew that to slow down or stop would mean my own demise. It was with a sadness that punched my chest that I left them to be consumed by the destruction I left in my wake.

Then, as I pulled away from the surging, splitting ground, a great crack came to my ears. I glanced back, and thought I saw something huge and pale emerge from the subsiding rock, as tall as a skyscraper and almost gleaming in the ghostly glow of the moon; it was only there for an instant, however, before a second, cacophonous noise shook the world.

A great boom threw clods of sandy soil and brown rock high into the heavens, a cloud of green-tinted dust spreading across the sky, sweeping over all light. It flowed up and outward, carried on a dreadful shockwave, faster than my little car could drive.

When it struck me, it blew out my windows, my tires, and my eardrums. In an unsettling silence I was thrown from the not-roads that led to Manhattan, car spinning, churning up great clods of dirt that battered me without a sound.

Then all was still.

I stumbled out of the corpse of my car and slumped down beside it. My eyes fell upon the barren waste that had once been Manhattan, where fierce fires now turned the dry dust to ash. What remained of the buildings became kindling to those flames, and it took less than a minute for the smoke to start dropping soot upon me, like little droplets of ashy rain.

That brings me back to the opening of this record. I haven't moved from the car since then; I only opened the trunk to retrieve what paper and pens I had left inside it. The grey snow is all that remains of Manhattan and Manhattan Mine. I only hope that whatever I saw attempting to emerge from the earth is gone too.

I cannot bring myself to face my pa, to tell him what became of his brother Bert and the town they had both called home. My book, too, seems so insignificant now, compared to what I have been forced to face. No doubt I am touched by the same madness that consumed the men and women of Manhattan; and if only I could have saved the boy!

Now that my testimony is complete, I shall stagger out into the dry, dust-choked desert. That shall be my purgatory; I shall wander until I expire, wearing my guilt like chains upon my ankles. Do not look for me. Only tell those who knew me that, though I failed to save this town from the madness in Manhattan Mine, at least that madman and his god of bones—whether real or not—will never trouble anyone else.

Signed,
Maxwell Otto Wolfe

ACKNOWLEDGEMENTS

Where to begin with the many thanks necessary for this, my second full book and first novella? There are so many people who have provided support and assistance in the formation of this tale.

First of all, it goes without saying that I owe much to my partner, Shannon. She not only endures my anxieties and self-doubts but supports me through it all. Hers are the first eyes on everything I write, and I can always count on her to be honest about what works and what doesn't.

She is also an inspiration to me, always.

Next, I owe a landslide of gratitude to my beta-readers, who gave this story so much praise whilst suggesting improvements. This story wouldn't exist as it does without your valuable input.

In no particular order, these wonderful readers—with Instagram tags alongside—are:

Derek Hutchins (@themanwhoknewjustenough)
Jack Harding (@rocket.man.reads)
Andrew Jackson (@authorandrewjackson)
Christopher Robertson (@*kitromero*)
Samuel M. Hallam (@*still_reading_sam*)

Megan E. Grey (@*m.e.grey*)
Alana K. Drex (@*alana.k.drex*)
Pan (@undead_dad_reads)
David Burchell (@*oldcataclysm*)
Lisa (@wordsandrecreation)
Peter Measures (@*manwhoam*)

Thank you all.

Appreciation also goes out to the incredible Writer's Circle I have the good fortune to be a part of. Our entertaining chats, deep discussions, and amazing network of support has fought off negativity and given me the strength to continue my writing career.

Plus all the other wonderful people of Bookstagram. It's such a great community to be part of. There are too many people to list here, but I've had some fantastic conversations, learned a lot from a diverse range of people, and discovered so many amazing books that I can't wait to read... eventually.

Though not necessarily fans of the stories I write, my family have always been immensely supportive of my writing ambitions. I may not always be the most attentive son, brother, etc. but know I appreciate you all. Without your encouragement I may never have dared to release my stories.

Further thanks go to you and all my readers. Whether this is your first time reading my work, or you came here after a journey Beyond Dimensional Veils, I am eternally grateful that you chose to read my words. After all, it is for the readers that stories are written.

Finally, a huge thank you to everyone who reviewed my short story collection. The praise and reception have encouraged me to continue writing, and I hope this book has proven enjoyable. I wish I could thank every reviewer individually.

If you enjoyed this book, please do leave a review on Amazon.

Last time I wrote an acknowledgements section, I promised that my last book was just the beginning of the horrors my mind has conjured. This time around, I can say "this is not the end". More is coming.

Until the next release, stay safe, stay spooky, and keep reading.

Kyle J. Durrant
2023

ABOUT THE AUTHOR

Kyle J. Durrant was born in 1997 and raised in East Anglia, though has probably spent most of his life exploring fantasy universes and macabre realities. He fell in love with writing at the age of ten and hasn't stopped since.

When not writing, he tends to sit in varying stages of existential dread, or delves into video games, books, and movies relating to whatever obsessive fixation he is in at the time.

Kyle has written copious amounts of notes relating to his fictional worlds, which drastically outnumber his completed stories.

Follow him on Instagram: *@kylejdurrantauthor*

*I dedicate this book to my mother,
Ulrica Y. Farmer*

Mistreated, But Loved

1.

Growing up, I was surrounded by nothing but love. Everybody loved me, I was their RAH. I was blessed to have the family that I had. I was spoiled and got whatever I wanted. It didn't have to be expensive or new. I appreciated it because, just like my great grandma Janice Mae would say, "They didn't have to do it for you. So, appreciate it."

I grew up in two separate households with my two grandparents, Grandma Ann (my mother's side), and Grandma J (my father's side). They lived in separate houses across the fence from each other in Whitehaven. I lived with my mom at her parents' home while my dad stayed with his mom. I went over to my dad's all the time, especially on the weekends. Grandma J raised me to be the person that I am today. She has never tried to replace my mother, but I knew Grandma J intended to up the slack my mother left behind. My parents were eighteen and nineteen when they had me, so as a grandmother should, she felt somebody had to raise the baby along with her own babies. Besides, I *was* her first and only grandchild.

My mom and dad got married the year after I was born. Of course, they loved each other, but like I said, they were young, and it didn't last very long. They separated before I turned three years old. They respected each other as growing adults and they never did let me see them fight. Regardless of the separation, we were still a family no matter what.

***

It was 1998, the year I would start kindergarten. This experience was new for me, but it looked fun enough to try. I attended Oakshire elementary, made good grades, respected my elders, and was one of the brightest students.

School was routine for me, but what wasn't, was my mother continuing to bring home her dates. One afternoon my mom introduced me to her new boyfriend, Randy. Out of all my mom's friends, Randy was different. He was bringing her stuff and even taking us out to eat sometimes. None of my mom's friend were coming over every day, but Randy was. The next thing I knew, we were all living together. I had my own room, but I didn't care. I just wanted to be at Grandma J's house. My big cousins were always there and most importantly, Grandma J and her family gave me all the attention I wanted. I ate good soul food every day. We all loved each other without being hateful. It was just a good place to be.

Randy and his family had their own restaurant called, "Mr. Johnson's Chicken & More", that was going great. He seemed to successfully take care of my mom and me. I believed he was rich, because of all the material things he had at home: big TVs, new furniture, jewelry. He even bought my mom a new car and gave her money.

The first time Randy and I went somewhere alone was when we attended the shrine circus. I had never been to any kind of circus before. I saw a clown for the first time and was a little scared, until I realized it couldn't hurt me. One walked up and made me a balloon puppy. Later we saw the huge elephants doing tricks, weird people moving their arms all the way around their heads, and more clowns running around making noise. Randy had even gotten me a big cotton candy stick, popcorn, and a red candy apple. I had fun but that still didn't make him my dad, right?

We eventually met his family and they accepted me and mom as their own. His mom and dad were still together, and they were kind people. Randy had four other brothers and a

Mistreated, But Loved

sister: Frank, Pun, Evan, Kevan, and Amelia. I called them my uncles and auntie. They loved football as a family; the Tennessee Titans were their favorite team. On Sundays, they would have dinner with most of their family, friends, and neighbors, to watch football games and eat. It sounded louder than a stadium full of fans. The men were cursing and drinking beers, having a good ole time in front of the big screen T.V. The kids would be upstairs with Uncle Kevan as we played the PlayStation, hide-go-seek, watched T.V, or went outside and played ball, running wild until it was time to go. Uncle Frank had four kids: Isabella, Frank Jr, Rico, and Kelly. Frank Jr, Rico, and I, were close in age, so we were around each other all the time. I guess you can say I had a new family.

Funny thing was, I didn't care how nice they were or how much fun we had, I still wanted to be at Grandma J's house at the end of the day. Everybody respected everybody, and there wasn't any 'baby daddy' drama. I always had fun with my dad. We went to Liberty Land and several arcade places in the city. He was a barber and took me with him, whenever he had custody of me. So, I went with him and had a great time, his clients were super funny and I laughed all the time. He always wanted to teach me different things and talked my ear off every now and then. The only weird thing was that Randy, and my dad had the same name. My mom must've loved them Randy's. I loved my dad so much. We had so much fun together. I couldn't wait to be with him. I was a daddy's girl for sure.

2.

It was the spring of 2000 and I was in Mrs. Jones first grade class. I had gotten into trouble because I was talking with another one of my classmates. That day, everybody in the class was talking, but Mrs. Jones decided to single me out. She was a mean old lady in a wheelchair; maybe in her late 40s. She was light skinned and always wore this real loud red lipstick with a lot of makeup. She always had a smug on her face, mean as a sailor. Her son would help her get out the car each morning and roll her into school in her wheelchair. She was even mean to him: like if she were having trouble getting out the car, she would yell at him as if it were his fault that she was having trouble. She also had a yardstick she carried all the time. If any of my peers or I were talking or something, she would sometimes tap our butts with it.

"Come here lil' girl, call your mama because you still talking," she would say with that yard stick in her hand.

I was raised to respect my elders, so without any complaints, I did. Even while I dialed my mother's number, I still tried to explain to her it wasn't just me. Sure, me and my classmates were talking, but we were *all* talking about what our parents were going to get us for our birthday's. Ms. Jones said be quiet to the group of us first. I didn't say anything else after that warning, but this kid John was still trying to talk to me!

I said, "Stop talking to me before we get in trouble."

That's when Ms. Jones called my name in that Cruella de Vile voice. She didn't care about what I was saying, she only cared about giving me a punishment. When my mom answered the

Mistreated, But Loved

phone, Mrs. Jones snatched the phone from my hands and started to babble. To this day, I still don't know what she told my mom.

Before I could return to my lessons that were assigned in class, my mother was already on her way. She had left her job, sped down to my school, marched inside, and knocked on the classroom door. When I saw her face through the glass, I was terrified. I swear, I hated getting in trouble because there were always consequences. My family believed in *whoopins'*, and I hated them.

My mom had this look on her face that told me I was about to be in big trouble. Her lips would squint in and she rolled her eyes constantly.

She said in a pissed and disappointed voice, "Come on here and you gone get it when you get home."

She held my hand so tight on the way to the car, I just didn't even say a word.

On the way home, she told me that Randy was going to whoop me. I was scared of the word "whoopin'" by itself. So, the fact that I was about to get one had my adrenaline going. I tried my best to stay away from getting a *whoopin'*, but I guess I ran into one that day. Randy had never whooped me before and I was so scared. I think I was more scared of how he looked. He was a big, buff, balled-headed dude. Who wouldn't be scared if they were my size?

When I walked in the house, my heart felt like it was already in my throat. My mom left out the door and went back to work.

In my mind I was saying, "Did she just leave me with him?"

I was so paranoid, even before the belt had touched me. It was now just me and him alone in that quiet apartment.

All of sudden he said, "Take off your pants."

I did with tears already coming down my face and my hands shaking.

Then he said, "Come here."

My heart was through the roof at this point. All I could think about was my dad and how I just wanted to be rescued.

I walked in Randy's room and he grabbed me. I was in one hand and the belt was in the other. He hit me one time,

Pop!

He gave me another,

Pop!

He was hitting me so hard that my skin started to rip. I was bleeding and my arms and legs had purple-red bruises. It looked like I had just been through a boxing marathon and I wasn't winning. I thought I was going to die. I had never felt anything this bad before. Nobody ever in my life, not even my own father, had violated me like that. This was a beating, not a *whoopin'*.

When it was over, I just cried and looked at my bloody bruises in disbelief.

As I was crying, the fool had the nerve to tell me "You better be quiet before I give you some more to cry about."

I just wanted my dad and Grandma J at that point. Luckily on Friday's, I went over to my dad and Grandma J's house. Randy had the balls to whoop me like that and then take me to my dad afterwards. It was quiet the whole ride, on the way to Grandma J's house. Randy dropped me off when the sun was going down. I bet he didn't give my dad time to look at me before he pulled off. Can you say Red Rum backwards?

When I walked in the house, Grandma J could tell there was something wrong.

She asked me, "What's wrong?"

I burst out into tears and said, "Randy whooped me and made me bleed."

She looked at my body and yelled for my dad to come and see. They took pictures of my bruises with a Polaroid camera for proof and then called the police. The police came the next day to take pictures and filed a report.

I'm not sure if they had talked to my mom or not because they sent me back over to her house like nothing even happen. At that point of my life, my spirit was beginning to break, and my feelings were corrupted. I was only six years old. I hated Randy for doing me like that. However, there was nothing I could do.

Shortly after that, Randy started to change for the worse. I'm talking change like Ike did Tina. One evening, Randy and I were leaving the apartment so that he could drop me off at Grandma Lee's house, his mother.

We were riding down the street and Randy said, "You don't like me, do you?"

I said, "No...no s-sir," in a soft, shaky voice.

He started talking loudly and cursing me out. I was so scared; I was only answering a question that he asked. I didn't say another word. I sat there with my hands in my lap, looking out the window.

Randy pulled his truck over on Raines and Hickory Grove Dr. and told me to get out of his truck. Why would he try to put me out on the side of the road? I cried and begged him.

"Please Mr. Randy, I'm sorry, I didn't mean to say that."

Mistreated, But Loved

He yelled "GET OUT!!"

I cried louder and said, "Please sir, I didn't mean it.

He said, "Naw, you think you grown telling me you don't like me, get out of my truck."

I said, "I do like you sir, I'm sorry, please!"

I felt like a prostitute begging her pimp while standing outside of the truck on the sidewalk. People were just driving by with their windows down. Nobody ever stopped to see what was really going on. I was hoping he let me back in or somebody would pull over to see why a little girl is standing outside a truck with a man in it, but no one came. It was about to rain, and the clouds were getting darker by the second.

He then let me back in the truck and told me, "Who you think you is, telling an adult you don't like them? I take care of you."

I was crying so hard that I turned red in the face and snot was pouring out my nose. I should've started walking but of course, I didn't know any better. I was only six years old.

At that age, I didn't know what to do or if I should tell anyone. Was I still going to Grandma Lee's house after all of that? That fool dropped me off over there like he didn't just try to abandon me on the side of the road. This *mane* was beyond crazy and I just wanted to be away from him. I was so frightened I didn't even tell anyone, not even my mother. In my mind, I was scared that he would tell people that I was lying. Later in life I told Grandma J what happened, but it was too late by then, I was already a teenager and that was in the past.

***

One night I was in my room asleep at the apartment. I woke up in the middle of the night because I had to use the

10

Mistreated, But Loved

restroom. I saw Randy standing in the doorway staring at me, but the crazy part was I didn't have a light on in my room. I could only see him because of the night light in the hallway. I was so scared; I didn't know if he was about to touch me or what. As I shuffled around in my bed, he knew I was awake, so he escaped to his back own room. When I tiptoed towards the bathroom, I made sure I locked the door. When I opened the door to go back to my bedroom, I looked both ways like I was about to cross the street. I couldn't really go back to sleep, so I turned on my tv until I drifted off. He never came back to the front by my bedroom, I guess he went on to sleep.

My mom and Grandma J had always told me, "If somebody try to touch you, you try to kick or grab their nuts and squeeze them as hard as you can and tell us for sure. We don't play that."

I was little but I was ready to protect myself. If he would've touched me, death would've been at his doorway quickly. Maybe he admired my beauty as a little girl or maybe he was just a sick, fuck.

He used to always say, "I want a little girl that look like you."

Whatever that meant. I was a bright child. I had light skin, pink lips, long, thick, curly hair, light brown eyes, and a pretty smile. He was just doing a lot of weird stuff.

***

Here it was my 2nd grade year at Oakshire Elementary, my favorite elementary school. We were a school of early scholars and they pushed us to be successful in our future. We had the best teachers, cafeteria food, a wonderful bookstore, and a delicious concession stand. My class used to have carpet time

Mistreated, But Loved

before we went home. Carpet time is when the teacher reads a book to the class or we would watch a movie until it was time to go home.

On this day we had combined classes with the lady across the hallway. I won an airhead candy during class earlier by answering questions. I had it in my pocket all day. Lunch was so good I forgot to eat my airhead.

When we got to carpet time, I ate my airhead. I didn't think anything was wrong. The teacher across the hall was watching over us and she saw me eating my airhead.

She got real upset and said in an angry voice, "I'm going to call your parents because you have no business eating on the carpet." She acted like I was doing something harmful. I didn't say a word.

She called my mom and all I felt was my heart racing. In that moment, I knew…Randy was about to get me again. She used to threaten me all the time when I did something wrong.

She would say, "You better stop before Randy comes and gets you."

I know she probably thought he cared about me and wanted to raise me well, but he was evil. Everything he did was because he wanted control. If he wasn't in control, he would be pissed. He would talk to anybody however he wanted to at the time. He respected who he wanted to respect and disrespected everyone else. He would even get violent sometimes.

I didn't go home after school. I was in after school care until my mom got off work. I didn't say much in aftercare that day, my stomach was so bubbly. I knew that when my mom picked me up, I was going to get a *whoopin'* by Randy. It's hard to have fun during the day knowing you are going to get in

Mistreated, But Loved

trouble at the end of the night. Especially when you know how bad you don't want the consequences to happen.

When she picked me up, I was trying to keep my composure and act normal. She had this disappointed look on her face, so yep, I already knew what time it was. We left the school and went directly up to the family business where Randy worked.

My mom and I walked in the restaurant and went straight to the back of the building. He was standing there in his work uniform smoking a cigarette like we were in a mob movie; his back turned. I was standing there looking like his prey that was about to be attacked. The tears were already coming down my cheek. He didn't say anything, he just grabbed me in one hand and his belt in the other. Maybe it was because of the force he was putting into the beating that made it so bad. It seemed like he put all his strength into it. We were outside in the back of the building, so I had room to run from the licks that were coming my way. Who wants to be bloody after a *whoopin'*? I ended up running the wrong way because I tripped in gravel rocks, mud, and dirty water. Randy still had the belt on my backside.

When he finished, I was once again bruised and bloody. This time really messed me up because my mom was standing right there when he was doing all this. Why would she agree to some man hitting her daughter like that? Maybe she thought because he provided, he had the right to. I was so confused. I couldn't agree because I had a father that had always been in my life, loved, and provided for me. He was in no way like Randy.

It was funny how every time he whooped me, I would go over to Grandma J's house the next day or so. When I got over to Grandma J's house, I didn't say anything about the *whoopin'*. I didn't have to say anything because after the last time he did this, she checked my body all the time when I came over.

She called my dad in the room and said, "Look at this on her!"

My dad stormed out the door. I had never seen him move so fast before. Grandma J tried to stop him, but he left so quickly. The police came and they did another report and took even more pictures. This time they called my mom over to talk about what was going on with me.

The police told my mom, "Ma'am, that man is not to put his hands on her again. He is not your husband nor her father."

She simply said, "Ok."

I still had to go back to that hell hole though. As time went on, I realized that I was going to be there for a while. Even though he whooped me until I bled, I still had to respect him. I lived in his house and I had to go by his rules. It was a forceful life to accept at a young age.

I said, "yes sir" and "no sir" and never gave him or my mother real problems to be harshly punished for.

Little did I know, Randy and my mother had problems as well. I wonder if she was just as scared as I was. What was he doing to her when I wasn't there? I mean, he couldn't just have been hateful towards me, right?

3.

Time went by and he started calling my mom any names he felt *whenever* he was pissed. I wanted to kill him at times but only to protect my mom. I just wanted him gone; out of our lives.

I started getting closer to Grandma Lee. I loved that woman like she was my blood. She treated me just like her own grandchild. I'd sometimes spend the night over her house. She'd cook big breakfasts and dinners. She always made sure I was full while I was with her. We would go up to Randy's family restaurant and have wings, fries, onion rings, fish, chicken tenders, and all kinds of good food.

I was taught how to cook, take orders and host. Grandma Lee was a great mother and wife who loved her family and God. She played the piano at church and she always wanted me to come play drums with her. I got to play a couple times on women's day at her church.

I couldn't believe this was the woman that raised Randy. They say train up a child in the way he should go and when he is old, he will not depart from it. I'm guessing he departed from it as he got older.

We lived in Autumn Ridge apartments. I was sleeping one night, and I woke up to a lot of yelling and screaming. It was Randy and my mom arguing. Why were they arguing? I didn't know.

He was yelling at her so much that I was starting to get scared. I thought he was about to hurt us both. I know the neighbors must

Mistreated, But Loved

have heard him because the walls were thin, and he was really loud. My mom rushed in my room to get me dressed so we could leave. While we were heading to the door, he snatched my mom keys and took her key off the keychain. He threw her keys back at her so hard, it looked like he was trying to pitch a strike.

I just wanted to know why he was doing us like that. I loved my mom so much, but she was nuts for being with him. I remember one time he made my mom change her clothes because he didn't like what she had on. He was very insecure. She would always be home because he also didn't like the friends she had. He really was trying to keep her to himself.

The situation was just dysfunctional and toxic. My mom and I went to Grandma Ann's and papa's house; they were my mom's parents. We stayed a few days, but after she calmed down, it was right back to Randy. Could it get any worse?

My mom's first cousin Tarletha came over one Saturday and they were in my mom's room trying on her clothes. They left me behind with Randy in the kitchen, but I wasn't going to have that. I was trying to go and join them just so I could get away, but Randy was trying to stop me.

>He was just a malicious, low down, evil human being.

>He said in a quiet, angry voice with his teeth clinched tight together, "Come here, don't go back there."

I tried to keep walking up the hallway, but he grabbed me, dragged me to my room, and roughed me up against the wall. He knew how to use his force against me in a way my mom wouldn't hear. I was only eight years old. I screamed for him to stop, and he let me go, running back to the kitchen like a mad man, in hopes that he wouldn't get caught by my mom and Tarletha.

Tarletha and my mom walked to my room quickly to see what was going on.

My mom and Tarletha both said, "What's wrong?!" with concerned looks on their faces.

I said, "He jacked me up on the wall!"

My mom said, "WHAT?!"

From the kitchen, he yelled, "No I didn't, stop lying on me little girl," his voice was always deep and aggressive.

Maybe my mom believed me but didn't do anything about it. I just wanted somebody to standup to him for me.

I kept thinking, "Somebody please come knock this negro out!"

I was hoping my mom would eventually leave him, but we kept on waking up every day…right there in his house.

My mom came to pick me up from school after her doctor's appointment one evening and she was crying. My after-school teachers loved my mom. They were genuine ladies who were concerned for her. As soon as my mom walked in, they knew something was wrong. She told them that she was pregnant, but her baby will have sickle cell. I didn't know what sickle cell was at the time.

When she calmed down, we left, and she told me I was going to be a big sister. I was happy because I was about to have a baby sister or brother, but I didn't want them to turnout just like Randy. Oh boy, was I stuck with him now.

It was a bittersweet moment. Despite everything, I couldn't wait for the little one to come. I wanted a little brother, I guess because of my rough ways. I thought, now I could have somebody to play with and throw around.

Mistreated, But Loved

I ended up getting a beautiful little sister, she was born in October 2001. She was born on Uncle Castro's birthday. We were having a party for him when Grandma Ann and others called with the news. I was so happy, I wanted to go see her right away.

The day she was born, was the first day I had ever seen Randy smile. Maybe he had a change of heart now that he had a daughter of his own. He was so nice and sweet to my little sister, that he even started being nice to me. Was this new life changing him? I sure hoped so because life was peaceful for everybody.

I loved my little sister, and her name was Kailey. Kailey was the brightest little thing, she looked just like me. I didn't want her to be like her dad point, blank, period. She had to be better. I wanted to be her Super Big Sis.

Randy was being so nice to me, he bought me my first bike without training wheels. He taught me how to ride it and everything. It was an all-purple bike with flowers on it and the pedals went back so I could burn rubber and make the tires slide when I stopped. I loved that bike so much. I washed it just like the adults washed their cars.

When Kailey was about five months, we moved into an actual house. It was cool. I had my own room again and Kailey had hers. We had a big screen tv in the living room with a PlayStation and PlayStation 2. We had access to all the channels on cable and the computer had internet. I didn't really get on the computer, but I eventually learned. My mom and Randy's room had a bathroom in it, and it had a huge jacuzzi. I really wanted to get in that thing right away! I liked the new house; it was very different from what I lived in before.

My Auntie Dora stayed across the street from us in some apartments. Auntie Dora was my mom's big sister, not to mention my favorite auntie. Auntie was always in my life. She used to take me to fun places like the zoo, arcades and anything a girl does with their auntie. She always had money, so anything I asked for, I got it. I was happy Auntie Dora didn't stay far from us because I knew she wouldn't let anything happen to me. Little did I know, auntie was already suspicious Randy was crazy.

4.

I left Oakshire and was transferred to Oakforest elementary during my 4th grade year. Oakforest was closer to the new house that we had moved into. I didn't want to leave Oakshire because all the friends I grew up with were there.

My younger cousin Tamar went to Oakforest with me, she was in 2nd grade. She would sometimes spend the night on school nights. Her mom and sister had to be at work earlier than we had to be at school, so my mom would take us to school and her mom would pick us up. However, once I started Taekwondo, that job was left to the afterschool bus.

Back then, we ate good after school all the time. We loved McDonalds, so that was always our choice for an afterschool snack. My mom and Tamar's big sister, Tamisha, were best friends since they were kids. We were basically inseparable. At the end of the day, we were more like sisters, than cousins. Even though we were two years apart, we were always on the same level. She taught me a lot of book work and helped me with my homework. Sometimes she just did it for me...she was smarter after all. She wasn't a little baby I had to look after like Kailey.

Tamar spent the night at my house one Thursday in order to do homework together. By the end of that long night, we had finished our homework, ate dinner and had taken our baths. It was getting late, and Randy got home while we were still up.

Randy said, "It's time for y'all to go to bed."

We said, "Yes sir."

Mistreated, But Loved

He then walked away as quickly as he came in, back to his room.

I told Tamar, "He so mean, I wish he never came home."

She said, "He *is* mean, I hate seeing him too."

We went on to my bedroom and we started to fall asleep, but the television was still on.

He then came into my bedroom and said, "Turn that TV off. Y'all need to go to sleep, I said!"

Half asleep, I quickly turned the television off. I usually had my television on every night before I would go to sleep. That's just how I slept. I watched TV every night to fall asleep. He's usually at work when I go to sleep, but he just so happened to come home early that night. I think he was having one of his outrageous episodes and wanted to control something and Tamar started crying shortly afterwards.

I asked her, "What's wrong Tamar?"

She said, "I'm scared of the dark."

So, I turned the television back on. Randy must of heard because he came back in my room with a very irritated voice saying, "Didn't I tell you to turn that tv off?"

I woke up in panic.

I said, "Yes sir, but Tamar said she's scared of the dark."

He didn't care at all.

Randy said, "Come here because you hardheaded."

I did.

My mom was in Kailey's room, getting her ready for the night. I wonder, did she hear any of this? I was hoping she did. I got to his bedroom, standing there with my night gown on. It was a

21

silk Tennessee Titans gown with the arms and legs out. He got that belt out and sure enough he started *whoopin'* me, one swing after another.

I was crying out from the painful licks, hoping my mom would hear me. Did it matter to her? I couldn't believe he was doing this again. I hated him so much.

My mom burst in the bedroom and said, "STOP, you not supposed to be whoopin' her!" No permission was giving this time.

I ran back in my room crying to myself. Tamar was scared because I was scared, and she kept telling me it's going to be alright. He didn't even whoop me long this time, but I still came out with nasty welts. Police clearly told my mom he couldn't put his hands on me anymore. It was two years later, and I was back at square one. I went on to sleep that night.

The next morning when we got up, my mom looked at my fresh welts. She said they weren't that bad. I didn't care how good or bad they were, this negro put his hands on me again. I was a respectful little girl, and I didn't deserve to be punished like that. *Was I that bad?* Maybe just in Randy's eyes.

We went on with the morning and she dropped me and Tamar off at school. I went to school all day with a jacket on. I didn't want any of my peers to make fun of me about my welts. Kids were mean and said cruel things and I didn't want anybody to say anything to me. It was just embarrassing to be picked on as a troublemaker.

***

I attended the Taekwondo University after school program. The bus came to pick us up from school. When I got on the bus, I took my jacket off. It was hot outside. I wasn't

Mistreated, But Loved

even thinking about my welts anymore, I was ready to have fun in after care.

My bus driver loved us like we were his own kids. He talked to us with kindness every day and we seemed to never get on his nerves. Mr. Will was his name.

> One of my peers said, "Mr. Will look at RAH's arms."

> He said, "Lord honey, what happened to you?"

> I said, "I got a whoopin' last night by my momma boyfriend."

Mr. Will was so upset, he turned red in the face. Mr. Will told me he was going to tell the after-care instructor about what I had just said.

> I said, "Please don't Mr. Will, I might get in trouble."

> He said, "If I don't say anything to the authorities, I could get in trouble just because I know about it. This is abuse." I sat there with a blank face and said, "Yes sir."

I didn't understand at the time what he meant. My aftercare was really concerned about me. They called the police to check everything out. The police called my dad and told him to come quickly. He was coming to get me anyway because it was Friday. My dad was so mad at what the police told him. He hugged me so tight and told me he loved me.

He talked to the police and they came to Grandma J's house the next day. When I got to Grandma J's house, I felt safe. All I wanted to do was be there and never go back to Randy's house. My mom came over that Saturday and the police had a sit down with her. The officer asked her a thousand questions and they all sounded like *blah blah blah blah blah.*

> I'm saying to myself, "Why are they talking to her, they need to go get him."

Mistreated, But Loved

By the end of the conversation, the officer said to my mom, "Ma'am, RAH will be staying here with her father and grandma for right now."

My mom was so mad, sad, and angry because there was nothing she could do. Deep down inside I was the happiest kid alive. I wanted to be anywhere else but in Randy's presence. I was where I wanted to be, which was Grandma J's house.

5.

I finished the rest of my 4th grade year at Oakforest. I transferred back to Oakshire my 5th grade year. All my friends lived in the neighborhood and went to Oakshire. My homies were happy I came back as well. We got to hang out every day instead of just on the weekend.

School was going well, and I was making A's, B's, and some C's. My conduct was never a problem. Whenever I had problems with homework or understanding something, Grandma J helped me. Her patience for me was huge. She made me read and when I came to some words that I didn't know how to pronounce, she helped me break the word down until I got it.

Grandma J was more than a grandmother, she was my teacher, hero, guide in life and not to mention my best friend. I was her only grandchild and she spoiled me like a daughter. She always reminded me that on the day I was born, she told Grandma Ann, "This one right here is my baby and the next one will be yours."

Grandma J and I grew a bond so strong, that I never wanted to be away from her. She was my safe-haven. I knew she would go beyond the earth to make sure I was taken care of.

If you wanted jokes and good vibes, Grandma J was the one. She was a very creative woman and she taught me to be the same. I wanted to be just like her; an outspoken, loving, smart, wealthy, happy human being.

She always said to me, "You are a leader, so you have to be the best RAH you can be. You represent your family, and we always honor and respect each other." That stuck with me for the rest of my life.

Mistreated, But Loved

Every Saturday all you heard was the blues coming from the W.D.I.A, A.M station and Uncle Castro chilling with his pall mall gold 100s and coffee mixed with Canadian Club whisky. The station had a special called, *All Blues Saturday.* They played all the oldies like B.B King, Johnny Taylor, Temptations and more.

It made my soul wise or what some called, an old soul. Uncle Castro and Nana were the cooks of the family. There was no telling what they were cooking but you knew it was going to knock you off your feet. It was something about how they cleaned and seasoned their meats and foods.

Uncle Castro always said, "You don't want to cook it too fast; you take your time so it's just right."

And boy was it RIGHT! I called it a taste from the angels. Even though Uncle Castro was my great uncle, he was my favorite uncle. He was Grandma J's older brother. He loved me like his own grandchild. One day I was moving around too much, after uncle had told me to sit down time after time. He pinched me and I turned red as a fire ball. He felt so bad about it.

He looked at me and said with a sad look on his face, "I'm sorry, I won't do that no more wookie."

I knew he meant it. I could see a little tear shed from his face. His eyes were a little wet and Nana and Grandma J kept laughing at him.

He kept rubbing my arm and saying, "Shit, I won't do that no more!"

He always said I was to light to do anything. That meant anything happened to me you will see it clear.

My great grandmother Janice or as I call her, Nana, was the sweetest lady I had ever met. She was Grandma J and Uncle Castro mother and my dad's grandmother. She loved everybody and everybody loved her. Everybody called her, "Big Momma" or "Aunt Janice". Her love for people was very Godly and real.

I never seen her so mad until Randy whooped me. I was questioning if this was the same woman. She does not play when it comes to her children. When I tell you, she will go to war with whoever over her children, she will.

Nana taught me to love my enemies and no matter what somebody else was doing, I needed to stay in my own lane.

She always said, "You gone be alright and just watch, they gone get it back."

I had so much wisdom around me and didn't even know it. Nana and Grandma J had raised my dad to be the man he is today. Even though his dad wasn't in his life growing up, he made sure he was a great dad to me.

My dad and I use to have the greatest times. We didn't need a lot of money to have fun. When he cut his clients hair on Saturday's, I would be right there with him. My dad used to take me to the skating rink, movies, museums, Putt-Putt golf and our favorite, celebration station. Celebration Station was a fun place for kids. They had Go Karts, bumper boats, a laser tag arena, good food, miniature golf, *Playland* rides, batting cages, and a whole lot more. It was better than any arcade I'd ever went to and we went *often*. I didn't care where we went, as long as I was with my dad.

I knew that once we finished having fun, we were going to eat anything I wanted. I loved pizza and burgers, plus the food at the house. I just had a ball all the time.

On Sunday's, Grandma J, Nana, dad and I would go to church. We went to Vernon Chapel in Rossville, TN. I'm talking early, like waking up with the birds chirping early. We went to the 8 a.m. prayer service, 9:30 a.m. Sunday School, 10 am Morning service and sometimes 2:30/3 p.m. evening service.

Growing up, I thought I had all the God a person needed. I loved church. I was involved in ministries at a young age. I was an usher on the youth and adult usher board. I was so dedicated to everything I started. I went to vacation bible school and revival for three nights every summer. You couldn't tell me I wasn't a saint. *The devil, where?*

I started playing drum set at the age of two. I used to beat on buckets, pots and pans. I became the church musician at the age of six and I was baptized at the age of seven. God blessed me to be a multitasker.

Our drummer at Vernon Chapel, Joe, passed away. My cousin Keys told me to get on the drums one Saturday at a funeral. I'm not sure if it was Joe's or not but I got on up there.

Keys played all instruments from the piano, organ, guitar, and drums. He was the greatest around me. He directed me on the drums while he was on the organ. He showed me what to do with my hands and I caught on at that very moment. It was incredible how me; a six-year-old girl was picking up on a beat and keeping the tempo right. Shortly after that, I realized nobody was playing the drums.

After church one Sunday, I asked Grandma J, "Is Joe coming back?"

She said, "No, he passed away."

I told her I wanted to play drums at church. Soon after that, I was the new musician of the church. I was not perfect, but it was the beginning, and I kept that tempo going.

I loved the drums so much; I would cry or catch a sad attitude when somebody had to play in my place. The deacons didn't let me play when we had evening services. I wasn't good as the

Mistreated, But Loved

experienced drummers, they said. I continued to be the drummer and I got better with practice.

My dad bought me a drum set like every three years because I would beat them to death. The drumheads would be busted and useless.

6.

Oakshire elementary 2003, was my last year of elementary school. I was so excited to be going to middle school. I had spent a lot of time away from Randy. I was so happy and enjoying life without being scared to do this or that and just being around him period. I didn't have anybody yelling at me because they were mad at the world. It was just a happy and loving time every day

Randy, Grandma Lee, and my family all were at my 5th grade graduation. It seemed like everybody was getting along as long as I was living with my dad and Grandma J.

First year of middle school was interesting. I attended Havenview Middle School, home of the Tigers. I played softball and I was in the orchestra; I played cello. I played basketball for a short period of time because I was lazy and didn't want to do those intense workouts.

My mom was supportive of me and I enjoyed her company. I enjoyed everything as long as I didn't have to live with Randy. I was still going over Uncle Frank and Grandma Lee's house sometimes. My dad didn't keep me from my mom, he just didn't want me living in the house with Randy.

I loved going over to Uncle Frank's house. I was going over Uncle Frank's house hanging out with Frank Jr. and Rico. They played football, so we always played with the football or played PlayStation. Rico was adopted; sometimes he didn't act like the rest, he was a wild child. Rico and I clicked the most. We used to do stuff that could've got me and him in trouble. We were sneaking out the house in the middle of the night, going to 18+ parties with fake ids, and we would even go the mall and he would steal from the store while I looked out for him. Our

Mistreated, But Loved

parents would've killed us. I was following him everywhere, knowing it was wrong.

My mom and them always said, "They are boys, and you are a girl. You have to be more careful."

But why? I didn't understand. My mom barely liked me going over Uncle Frank's house, but I kept going. Uncle Frank and Auntie Shannon didn't care what we did, as long as we were careful. Kailey would hang around Kelly, that's Frank Jr. and Rico's younger sister.

Rico was a bold little guy. I spent the night over there sometimes. We snuck out of the house some nights and rode bikes to his girlfriend's house or whoever's house. It was always two or three in the morning. I was so curious, following this mane in the neighborhood in the middle of the night.

The funny part was that the bikes were not even fully pumped. We were riding around on almost flat to the ground tires. He was desperate to sneak out and I was just going along like a dummy. We never got caught and I can't lie, it was fun but scary. I'm knowing good in well I don't like getting in trouble. Rico did eventually get caught. This *mane* hit the house backing out the driveway stealing Auntie Shannon Toyota Camry. He was caught red handed. It was no denying or covering that up. I'm just glad I wasn't with him that time. Rico and I use to watch tv late at night and we always seen this commercial with girls in bikinis, laying down in a big bed, on the phone. The girls were talking seductive saying, "Call this number now if you want to meet."

It was called, *The Chat Line.*

We were only eleven and twelve years old, calling such a number. We saw it at the end of the screen and decided why not…*just call it.* We listened to everybody's conversation in the chat rooms. We even talked to some girls. The chat line was very discreet. Nobody knew us and we didn't know anybody, except this one time I could've sworn I heard one of my older cousins talking. I hung up the phone so fast.

You would think I would've stopped getting on it but that didn't stop us, we continued to get on when we could. It was just very interesting to kids experimenting life. Rico was my best friend, cousin, and we talked about everything.

He talked about how Uncle Frank treated him, and I talked about how Randy treated me. We both felt the same way about those two.

We did get in trouble with a certain situation, or shall I say I got in trouble. I cat-fished some people. Technology was just coming out with new social media websites. Myspace was just surfacing, and it gave us a chance to be who we wanted to be, and no one knew the truth unless we wanted them to. I was on Myspace all day and night, changing my background layout and changing codes so my page was fresh or nice for everybody to see. Not to mention, I was being somebody I wasn't. Only Rico and I knew what I was doing.

Partaking in the biggest secret of my life.

7.

It was 2005 and my mom and I were riding down the street. Even though I didn't live with her, she came and got me sometimes on the weekend.

She said to me, "Things are going to change, you will be living back with us next year."

I swallowed my whole mouth. I was trying to grasp what she said because it was very disturbing to my ears. I was about to be twelve years old, and I didn't want to be back in Randy's presence. We were having a good relationship not being around each other. What was my mom trying to prove?

After a couple days, I didn't think about it like that no more. I was in denial; I did not want this to happen at all. The whole summer, my mood was up and down. I didn't want that happening. They still lived in the same house on Regency Place.

When I got there, it seemed the same to me. He was still quiet unless he was talking to his friends about ESPN or football. I said hey and I answered any questions he asked like did you do the dishes? Did you clean your room? Did you vacuum? Can you cook your sister some food?

I found out that Aunt Dora was living there while I was with my dad. Randy and Auntie Dora got into arguments almost all the time. He had the nerve to curse her out, but she wasn't going to take that, she cursed his ass back out. Auntie moved shortly after she saw how crazy he was and how her sister was changing. She got fed up with the craziness and pettiness. She didn't move far though. She moved back in the apartments across the street.

Mistreated, But Loved

  She used to always tell me, "I wish I had enough money to take you away from that evil man." For some reason I always hoped she would get that money to take me away.

I was transferred to Ridgeway Middle School my 7th grade year and finished middle school there. I was involved in activities at Ridgeway. I joined the choir, played the drums, and took up softball. I wanted to be at school or anywhere just so I wouldn't have to be around Randy.

Kailey had even grown up a little, she was now four years old. When I left school, I came home and had to baby sit Kailey until my mom got off. Randy had to be at work at 4 p.m. When he left home every day, I felt free. I got to talk on the phone, be on the computer and play my music loud.

  My mom and Randy assigned me chores. I washed the dishes, cleaned the kitchen, washed the clothes, vacuum all the rooms, and cleaned my room and bathroom. Kailey was a smart little girl. We didn't always see eye to eye. I think it was because Randy was her dad, and she knew how me and his vibe was. Plus, I had been missing for a few years too, so we didn't grow up in the same environment. She loved her dad, but I didn't. He was so sweet to her, I just wanted him to treat me like the way he treated her. They called each other buddy and had special handshakes. Kailey even got her first cell phone at the age of three. What could she do with a cell phone? I didn't even have a cell phone and I was about to be a teenager. Why didn't he treat me like that? I was here first, and I didn't do anything to him but respect him. I knew he wasn't my dad but what did that have to do with treating me like a human being?

  I was told, "You gone watch your sister until your momma get home and don't open the door for nobody." I followed the rules. Sometimes I would have to force Kailey to stay in the house because she didn't want to be there with me.

Mistreated, But Loved

Our relationship was a love/hate roller coaster. I didn't care how much we didn't bond like that, if you mess with her, you mess with me.

***

My mom had friends with kids. I got along with all of them, but my favorite was Tyesha. Tyesha was my ride or die. She was two years older than me. Our moms were great friends. I loved to be around their family. We used to spend the night with each other and had so much fun. Tyesha was more like the big sister I never had. We got on each other's nerves but couldn't stay mad for long. When Tyesha came over, my mom always went grocery shopping for snacks and food. We both ate like grown folks with big stomachs. We ate at the family restaurant sometimes too; I always got the ten-piece honey gold wings with fries and a large drink.

We watched music videos all day and night. She wanted to be a model and I wanted to just be on television. We used to record each other. Our greatest hit was when we did MTV cribs. We literally pretended we was doing MTV cribs at my house. She was recording and I was telling everybody what was going on.

Tyesha didn't like Randy either, I mean who did? He didn't have to say anything, his presence in the room made you not want to say anything to him.

Tyesha and I were watching tv one night when Randy walked in from work.

He said, "Y'all not gone speak to me when I walk in?" with his forehead wrinkled and eyes bucked.

Tyesha and I looked at each other with blank faces. It was weird because my mom just told Tyesha and I earlier that day, "When y'all walk in a room, you suppose to speak first because you are new to the room." So, in a respectful, soft tone I said, "My mom

Mistreated, But Loved

said when you walk in a room, you supposed to speak first because you are new to the room." Tyesha agreed. Why did I say anything at all?

He yelled back at me and Tyesha saying, "THIS MY MOTHER-FUCKING HOUSE, YOU SPEAK TO ME WHEN I WALK IN!"

My mom was in the room asleep.

She came in there with the sleep still in her face and said with an annoyed, loud voice, "What's going on?"

He was walking towards his room hollering at my mom, "THIS MY HOUSE…"

My mom cut him off and said, "Naaaaaw, I told them that's how it's supposed to be."

He got even more pissed off and started cursing her out. They were in their bedroom by that time. Tyesha and I were listening to make sure he didn't try to harm my mom. For some reason when Tyesha was around, I felt like I was tough enough to stand up to him. I knew her mom was crazy and probably would've sliced Randy apart. If he would've did anything that night, me and Tyesha was going to beat him senseless.

She had finally saw what I was going through, the crazy side. Why was he so demanding?

My mom's voice kept repeating in my head, "Things will be different this time."

I knew that was crap talk. The only thing that was different, was he wasn't physically touching me, he was touching me both mentally and emotionally…he was everywhere. When he yelled, it sounded like a demon was coming out of him.

I was on the computer one day after school and he was trying to tell me to do something and all I heard was, "Before I take off my belt." I had to remind him, I said in a soft, scared but in a respectful voice, "The police said you can't whoop me no more because you're not my daddy." Why in the hell did I say anything?

He got so freaking mad, he yelled, "WHAT!! IM GROWN LITTLE GIRL. THIS MY DAMN HOUSE. WHO YOU THINK YOU TALKING TO? I CAN DO WHATEVER THE FUCK I WANT TO DO. I PAY THE DAMN BILLS. WHO YOU THINK YOU ARE? YOU DON'T PAY NO BILLS."

My heart was beating so fast, I jumped back one time because I thought he was about to swing his hand. I stood there with tears coming from my face. I was scared of how loud he got, it felt like punches. I thought he was about to pull the belt out, but he didn't. If he would've pulled that belt off and tried to hit me, I probably would've tried to run. I was not about to let him touch me again.

He stormed out the house after he finished going off. I guess he just tried to scare me because old Randy would've pulled the belt out. I wasn't little RAH no more. Even though I wasn't stronger than him, I was going to put up a fight. That was the last time I cried over his words. I told my mom what happened, and I guess she handled it. I'm not sure.

8.

It was 2006, my 8th grade year. My mom asked me did I want to talk to somebody, like a psychologist. I didn't really want too, but she insisted it would be good for me. I ended up going to Dr. Frances. She was a great psychologist; she didn't judge me at all.

When I first started going, I didn't tell her too much. I didn't trust her; I didn't know her. However, I made sure I told her that I didn't want to be over there with Randy. I wanted to be with Grandma J and dad.

My mom was curious about me, she said I didn't show any emotion and I was always quiet. I wasn't a quiet person. I just didn't say too much around her and Randy. I didn't want to be around at all. It was just this feeling I had every time I walked in his house or when I was around him.

***

My mom started having bad headaches. They were so bad she used to get irritated and sleepy. She finally went to the doctor and found out she had a tumor on her brain. The tumor was big as a nickel and that wasn't good at all. She came to me and told me she was going to have brain surgery. I was confused because I never heard about anybody having surgery on their brain. I was worried about her every day. Her surgery was coming soon. I used to listen to her talk on the phone and she would say how scared she was. She didn't know I was listening, but that made me scared too.

When the day came, my stomach felt funny the whole day because she was about to have her procedure done. It was

Mistreated, But Loved

November 6, 2006. November was the month that something bad happened in my family. She was so worried and that made me worry too. I just wanted to be by her side through the whole process. I felt like if I were standing there the doctor would know not to play with me or her. I was with Auntie Dora after school that day. We were sitting in the waiting room. I kept looking for the doctor to come because I wanted to know if she was alright. I heard a noise coming down the hallway. It was the nurses pushing my mom down the hallway in her bed. They were pushing her at a fast pace. I thought something was wrong. They were trying to hurry up and get her to her room. Aunt Dora and I were walking fast with them. Aunt Dora said, "It's over." My mom was halfway sedated, and her voice was dragging. She kept asking Aunt Dora, "What they say? What they say?" Aunt Dora said, "Everything went great. Thank God." She stayed in the hospital a week in a half before coming home.

Everybody kept telling me I was going to have to help her, and things weren't going to be the same. I had to help my mom a lot because she couldn't do a lot for herself. The back of her head was stapled together from the surgery and she couldn't really bend or turn her neck normally. Seems like after her surgery, we started getting into arguments and disagreements. The better she got, the more she was getting on my case about stuff. I was not liking her attitude. She was tripping about things that she never tripped about, like wanting me to get off the phone at 8 when it was always 10p.m. She didn't want me to go out with my friends. When Kailey said I did something, she believed Kailey over me. I just felt a little unwanted. She didn't even want me talking to my cousin LaToni because she was a lesbian.

 I had grown a closer relationship with my older cousin LaToni on my daddy's side. LaToni was a lot older than me but we were related. My mom didn't know how close LaToni and I had gotten until she started hearing me say her name on the

Mistreated, But Loved

phone. My mom thought my cousin was trying to influence me to be a lesbian but that wasn't the case. I just enjoyed talking to a lot of my cousins and LaToni was one of them. I saw her at a family function, and I got her number and we have been talking ever since. I was comfortable saying and doing whatever I wanted to around LaToni because she wasn't judgmental. I was still figuring myself out in who I wanted to date, and my cousin LaToni was the only one I was comfortable talking to about it. I couldn't tell my mother that though. She would've been disappointed.

My mom told me that I needed to get off the phone and I was confused as to why. I wasn't doing anything wrong but talking to my big cousin. I told LaToni I had to get off the phone. I can't lie, I was upset, but my mom and I got into a heated argument about LaToni being too old to be on the phone with somebody my age. I was trying to figure out why did it matter; she was my cousin.

I packed my things in a backpack and stormed out the door. The only thing that was in the backpack was a cellphone. I had a cell phone nobody knew about but my friends. I walked out the house down the street. She said in a sarcastic voice," I'll see you later." I said in a soft, mad voice, walking away, "No you not." When I got to the end of the street, I called my dad and told him what happened. He asked where I was, and I told him. I was at a wing spot on Winchester between Kirby Parkway and Ross road.

My dad came in a hurry. He called my mom to see what had happened. My mom said to him, "You need to bring her on back." She called the police and told them I ran away. As bad as he didn't want to take me back, he did. He kept saying, "Just do what your mom tell you baby, you won't have to deal with this for long. I hate this but it won't be forever." I cried to him, "Please dad, don't take me back." I knew he had no choice

Mistreated, But Loved

though. We pulled back up to the house, my mom was waiting on me to get out. She had a belt. I got out the car and tried to walk in the house. My mom swung at me but something in me said, "protect yourself." I didn't swing but I tried to get her off me. I was so angry on the inside, but I didn't want to hurt her with her neck and all. My dad got out and broke it up, by that time the police were pulling up.

Next thing I know Grandma J and a few of my cousins pulled up. My mom was so upset that they came. I'm pretty sure my dad called them, but it wasn't to be messy or petty. More than likely he called them to see who could get to me first. The police got out their cars to see what was going on and told my folks, "Y'all have to leave because this not y'all's business." I was there with the officers and my mom. Both officers were black women, so I knew this wasn't about to be good for me. They are going to believe everything the mother says. This is not something I wanted to be doing with my mom, but she was really tripping.

Randy was at work and it seemed he either couldn't come home, or he didn't want to deal with it. He didn't show up at all. This wasn't his business either, plus he still wasn't married to my mom.

The police told me, "You got two choices, come downtown with us or take this whoopin' from your mom?"

I begged them, "I'd rather go downtown with y'all than to be here with her. Please take me with y'all."

They told me, "Naw, you gone take these licks from your mom, we don't want you to go to a juvenile detention center."

I wanted to be under the jail rather than being in the house with them.

Mistreated, But Loved

In my mind I'm like, "Is she really about to hit me? She still healing."

The officer was playing games. How you give me options and choose for me? I couldn't trust anybody, not even the law. If they only knew what I had been through in the past.

The officer said, "Turn around and put your hands on the wall."

They gave my mom one of their belts. My mom gave me five licks to my back side. *Yea, with her hitting me like that, she was healed if you asked me.*

The officer told my mom, "Hug her ma'am and tell her you love her."

I was full of rage at that very moment. I wanted her to get her hands off me. I know she didn't say she loved me. Lady please. I even wanted them officers to disappear off earth.

My mom then put me on the worst punishment ever. I couldn't talk on the phone or get on social media. Those were my two favorite things to do every day. All of this because I was talking on the phone with my cousin, and she is a lesbian? I was on punishment for a while, but I still did what I wanted to do when Randy or mom wasn't around, which was talk on the phone and be on Myspace. I was going over my dad's house on weekends anyway. I wasn't on lock down over there because I wasn't disobedient. Things got better after I got off of punishment.

9.

My 8th grade year was over, and my summer vacation had finally begun. I was able to spend it over Grandma J and Grandma Ann's house. My family had a BBQ, and we were all talking and joking around with each other. My cousin LaToni came over and she rarely comes to family get togethers. My folks say she's just an introvert, but she really means well. My mom wasn't sweating me, and I could talk on the phone all night if I wanted to. I even started hanging with LaToni a little bit. My mom didn't even know. I wasn't doing anything wrong though, just hanging with my cousin.

I was a tomboy, so people didn't know if I was interested in girls or boys. LaToni saw how I was dressed and how I carried myself and she was expressing how she goes to the LGBTQ clubs and about her lesbian friends. I guess she expressed herself to make me feel more comfortable. I mean nobody in my family knew too many lesbians. It was usually a secret. I was telling her that I have lesbian friends and they were cool to hang around, so I wanted to hang around her especially since we don't see each other. She told me we could hang out, but I wasn't old enough to go to clubs. I just said okay because I knew I was too young; I was fourteen at the time. She had a girlfriend named Brittany and Brittany had a sister named Brianna. Brianna and I were the same age and became close. She told me her darkest secrets and told me I was a great person to be around and a great listener. So anytime I was going around LaToni we were just hanging out with Brianna and Brittany.

We ended up hanging out almost every other weekend and we talked every day. She was just one of those cousins that let their little cousin get away with things. Word got around the

Mistreated, But Loved

family that I was hanging around LaToni and somehow it got back to my mom. Somebody was snitching. Why did my folks have something to say? My mom thought I was around a bad influence because she was a lesbian but that has nothing to do with her character.

LaToni and Taylor were my big cousins, but Taylor was my *big* cuz. She used to babysit me and call me her baby. Taylor knew more about LaToni than I did because they grew up, went to school, dated, and partied together. Taylor acted like she didn't want me hanging around LaToni because I was too young. I guess she thought LaToni was a bad influence like my mom. I was starting to think that Taylor was a little fake. It made me feel like she was playing both sides because as she was speaking negative about LaToni she was still hanging around her. Taylor told Grandma J that LaToni was trying to influence me to like girls, which was not true. I know she wanted the best for me, but I didn't understand why she told Grandma J that LaToni was trying to turn me out though. Most of all, why did she say it behind LaToni's back if they were so close? Made me think, she probably was a lesbian too.

It was so much drama going on with people telling my mom lies about the things I did and said. It was a lot of 'he say', 'she say' about my cousin trying to influence me to be a lesbian. I knew they didn't know what they were talking about and I was angry at the fact that my mom didn't believe me and believed those haters and bitter folks. My mom thought I was being influenced by a lesbian, so she felt like I needed to see a psychologist.

***

It was Saturday and I was at Grandma J's house. My mom called me out on some B.S again.

She said, "You over there being free and still doing what you want to do. I'm about to come pick you up and you coming back home with me."

I said, "What you talking about? I'm not doing nothing."

She said, "You still talking to that girl on the phone, and I told you to stop. You hard-headed. Your dad and grandma let you do anything over there."

I was so angry. I started rubbing my mouth and shaking as she was talking.

I said back to her on the phone, "I ain't going nowhere with yo ass!"

I hung up so fast then threw the phone on the bed like I was trying to break a rock. I wanted her to feel the damage through the phone. I was shocked at myself, but I was angry, deep inside.

I thought, "You just cursed at your mom."

I didn't care at the moment though. Grandma J was listening to me talk the whole time. She didn't want me disrespecting my mother, so she kept telling me to calm down and don't ever talk like that to my momma.

She said, "That's your mother and you have to be respectful."

I was so upset, I said to Grandma J, "She is just trying to ruin my life. How can she keep me away from my cousin?"

She said, "You can't be acting like that with your momma because she don't need to come over here with that shit. Your daddy is here and don't nobody need to be fighting or having a big misunderstanding over this. Now calm yourself down and you need to apologize to her when she get here."

Mistreated, But Loved

I said with an irritated voice, "Yes Ma'am."

***

My 9th grade year was approaching, and I was about to be fourteen. I had been ready for the parties and high school events. High School was a different vibe. I was fresh meat and shy out of this world. I went to Kirby High School and I was in J.R.O.T.C. I joined the unarmed drill team and stayed on it until I graduated. We had practices, competitions and I was very engaged with them. We loved each other like a family. We had some of the best memories with each other. I did color guard for football games and I marched in the Veterans Day parade downtown every year. It felt like Mardi Gras In Memphis, but we had cold weather. Rifle competitions were the best. I shot great targets and not to mention I was the only girl on my team. We had drill competitions in different states and in the city. Our favorite one every year was the Ripley, TN competition because some of the best J.R.O.T.C. teams were there from around the country. If we won against them then we were undefeated. We won overall 1st place my first year competing at the Ripley competition.

I went over my dad's one weekend and came home to my mom, Kailey, and I packing our stuff. My mom was finally leaving Randy. We moved into the apartments across the street, where Aunt Dora lived. It wasn't far from him but we weren't physically with him. Was my mom finally leaving him for good? I surely hoped so. Everything was going well. My mom gave me my first legit cellphone for my birthday. I was so happy, it felt like my first car. She needed to stay in contact with me and I loved to talk on the phone anyway. I gave everybody my number.

46

Mistreated, But Loved

I didn't stay far from school. I either got dropped off at home, Aunt Dora's house, or my friend's house after school. I was just glad I wasn't going to Randy's house. I was going over Grandma J's house on the weekends and coming back home to peace. Nobody liked Randy, so everybody was glad my mother was moving on.

My mom had start seeing this guy she knew from high school. He was the maintenance man in our apartment complex, and he stayed in them too. I knew for sure she was moving on now because the new guy, Miko, was making her laugh and he was doing things for her. He was making her laugh, giving her money, and fixing stuff in the apartment for free. Who comes to a tenant at midnight to fix a sink? Someone who has a crush on my mom, I guess. She usually doesn't bring a man around me unless she likes him seriously. I hadn't seen another man in her life besides my dad and Randy.

We were struggling but he was helping a little bit. I wasn't trying to be cool with no dudes my mom was talking to. Nope, not after Randy's crazy self. He ruined it for the future dudes my mom would talk too. Randy was mean and controlling and I didn't want another man coming in doing that anymore.

In the mornings, my mom dropped Kailey off over at Randy's house. He took her to school because she didn't have to be there until 8:30 a.m. I had to be at school at 7:15 and my mom had to be at work at 7:45. The feeling of pulling off from his house every morning was wonderful. I would look at him and the house and shake my head. I smiled every morning we dropped Kailey off. I enjoyed being at school, it was an escape from reality. I had peers to talk to and we were clowns anyway. We joked, laughed, and even talked about personal things. I wasn't the only one that had gone through something at home. Some people were getting abused by their own parents. I had my dad and Grandma J to look forward to. They didn't have anybody

Mistreated, But Loved

helping them, just stuck. I felt so bad for them because their story was worse than mine.

10.

It was November 2007 and things were getting weird. My mom found out Miko had a wife, and he was playing both sides. His wife somehow got my mom's number and called to spill the news. She didn't stay with him after that. Miko ended up being a crazy dude after all. He was stalking my mom and she had to get a restraining order on him.

One morning while dropping Kailey off, Randy brought my mom some breakfast to the truck. That's cool, don't nobody care about no breakfast. The next morning, he brought her breakfast again. He did this every morning for a week. He was being super nice. *Heavy on the super.* I have never in my life seen him be so catering. He even wanted me to come over because he cooked my favorite food. I ended up going over there with him one night and he did cook. *Randy was cooking dinner on a weekday?* I couldn't believe it. He had lost so much weight and his attitude was different. My mom said he was depressed. I didn't understand what depression was at the time.

He was talking to me about how he missed my mom.

He said, "I want y'all to come back, so we can be a family."

Wait a minute Randy, say what?

He was talking a good game too. He asked me about the dude my mom was talking to. I didn't know he knew about him. I guess my mom was serious if Randy knew. I wondered, did my mom leaving him teach him a lesson? I was only fourteen, what did I know about love.

Mistreated, But Loved

I went to my session with Dr. Frances the following week. My mom and I had a private session with her. I told them how he was being super nice and how he wanted us to come back.

My mom says to me, "If you're ok with us moving back with him, then we will. If you are not ok with it, we will not go back."

This was tough because I actually liked this Randy and he said he wanted us to be a family again.

I looked her dead in her eyes and said, "We can go back."

I couldn't believe myself after all the times I said I wanted to get away from him. He made it clear to me that he changed though, right? Maybe I was just like my mom, brain washed and confused. What was I holding on to? I couldn't answer myself. Even though I thought he'd change, I felt I messed up when we actually stepped foot back in the house. I should've told my mom *NO*. My mind was definitely playing tricks on me.

It was football season again and we started having Sunday dinner at the house again. Everybody was there from my family, friends, and neighbors. After the game was over, Randy proposed to my mom. I was shocked, I guess Randy did want his family back. I just wanted my mom to be happy and to be treated correctly. I wasn't worried about him *whoopin'* me or saying anything to me out the way anymore. Randy and I were cordial, I didn't say too much. Even though we had dinner and we talked, I still felt like I made the wrong decision. I didn't know what to say after all those years of being talked to and treated crazy. Believe it or not, I wanted to believe he was nice. I wanted him to be nice and treat me like he treated Kailey. I wanted to believe his attitude had changed completely and forever. Things sunk in after I parted my crazy lips to say those words. I know he talked about wanting his family back so I

Mistreated, But Loved

figured he wouldn't mess it up again. Talking crazy was his problem in the first place and not to mention how he whooped me.

They got married quick, it was April 2008. The wedding was beautiful, and everything was great.

I was standing at the altar saying to myself, "Don't say nothing RAH, this is not your wedding."

A part of me wanted to walk out but hey this was it. Randy was cool for the time being. He wasn't being mean, but I continued to think back on all the things he had done. I was trying to forgive him. If he asked me to do something, I just respected him now as my stepdad. No, I did not call him dad, he was still Mr. Randy to me.

The week of the honeymoon, I stayed over Uncle Frank's house. Frank Jr went to Kirby with me. Uncle Frank took us to school, and we'd walk back. Uncle Frank and Auntie Shannon didn't care about no curfew, you could basically be out all day and they weren't going to say anything.

My two homegirls Bria and Rita stayed close by, so we walked home together that week. My folks always told me to stay away from gangs, but I was experiencing. It was a Tuesday; me and my girls were walking home. My girl Rita was a Vice Lord and she wanted Bria and I to join.

I said, "Rita I'm not trying to fight to be in no gang."

Rita said, "You can get blessed in, you don't got to fight, I got you fool and plus we not a gang, we a organization."

I said, "What is blessed in?"

She said, "You gone see, I wouldn't let nobody hurt you and if yo momma boyfriend try something, we got protection for you."

Mistreated, But Loved

I trusted her because she was my home girl and if Randy started getting crazy again, I had protection. Rita knew how Randy could be so she figured this would help me in her mind. Me and Bria agreed to join.

The next day we walked home, Rita told me and Bria to come behind this abandoned house not far from the school. We had to meet this boy named Chi. He was the chief of the Vice Lords in the area. She told me this is the person who will be blessing me in. The house was boarded up and gang signs were spray painted everywhere. I couldn't understand what they said. As we walked to the backyard, I saw broken glass, trash, and even used condoms.

I thought to myself, "What young lady opened her legs back here?"

It looked like an empty drug house. I wasn't scared, but I was definitely thinking *eww*. Bria and I went on to the backyard and Rita held our belongings. There were twelve people with us, and they all stood in a circle surrounding Bria, Chi and I to be witnesses. This was some movie type stuff. Chi then told us to lift our hands. We had our hands up and he told us to look in his eyes and repeat after him. I didn't know what I had said after I finished. I wasn't serious about knowing this knowledge at all. When we were done, we were officially Vice Lords.

In my mind, I'm like, '*This it?*'

Chi told me he was going to get me my knowledge papers and I needed to study my history about the organization/gang. I didn't know I had to learn history and stuff like that. I barely like history at school, so I knew I wasn't about to sit and learn this knowledge.

It wasn't even a month later when Bria and I got called into the principal's office. Our "supposed to be friend" Greg was tripping. Rita, Bria, Greg and I were all friends. We all

Mistreated, But Loved

thought Greg was gay. He came to school one day and told people he had sex with Bria. When we heard the news, she confronted him, and I was right there on her side. He told the principal we were trying to start trouble with him. A bunch of lies he told. We are girls and he a whole dude. Sound kind of soft to me. Did he really go to the office on us? He even told the principal that we were in a gang and who our leader was. Wow Greg!

The principal went through our things and he found gang related stuff in Bria's folder. He was convinced we were in the gang now.

Before we left out of the office, he told us, "If anything happens to any of y'all, all y'all getting in trouble."

When we left out the office, we saw Chi in the hallway. Bria and I told him we just had left the office and that Greg was snitching. He said he was going to take care of him. Whatever that meant.

I'm fourteen years old, talking about, *I got a leader*. I was raised better than that but oh well, I was in it now. I wasn't walking home anymore but Rita, Bria, Chi and Greg were. I got a phone call from Rita and Bria an hour after I got home from school. They got on the phone sounding all sad and concerned. Rita said on the way home, Chi beat up Greg. He started having a seizure and blood was rushing from his head. The ambulance was called, and he was quickly rushed to the hospital. I'm glad he didn't die but that ass whoopin', yes, he needed it. I wasn't feeling all that bad, I couldn't be fake about it. They felt like since I didn't care, they could blame it on me.

Bria said to me, "You told Chi that Greg was talking about him in the office." In reality we both did.

I said to Bria, "You act like you wasn't the main one talking in the office or to Chi. We wouldn't even be in this situation if it wasn't for you. We wouldn't even have had beef with Greg if you wouldn't have said he made a rumor about y'all having sex. I'm taking up for you and you taking up for him. That's real fake Bria."

She didn't say anything after that. Rita was still on three way listening, saying in a soft voice, "Mmmhm," but she didn't say anything else. I knew that now; I was in a messy situation.

My parents were informed, and they weren't pleased at all. They raised me better than some gang, but this was my life. My dad was so upset, all I remember him saying is, "You around here in gangs and shit, like you don't have a family that love you." He was always happy and laughing, so to see him pissed was so disappointing. I never wanted to disappoint my family, I did know better, I was just making irrational decisions. I surely thought my mom was going to put me on punishment, but she didn't. She was disappointed and told me I need to start praying because I was becoming rebellious like. I guess when people heard gang, they automatically think NEGATIVE, which in most cases are.

I joined Vice Lord to be with my homegirls and have protection. Greg was out of school for the rest of the school year, Rita and Bria didn't want to be friends with me anymore and Chi said he was flipping to be a blood. He said I could either be blood with him or I didn't have to be nothing. I chose the neutral route: being myself, not being in any gang or click. A normal person living an average life again. I didn't have to worry about all this trouble and drama when I wasn't in a gang.

11.

It was summer 2009 and school just let out for the school year. I wanted to spend my whole summer over Grandma J's house instead of just weekends. I had more fun and love over there. I went to church and played drums on Sunday. I'd been playing there since I was five. My grandma took me anywhere she went. I ate all day and didn't have to ask permission to eat anything out the kitchen. If it was there, I ate it. I felt free and at home.

Grandma Ann stayed across the fence so if I wasn't at Grandma J's house my friends knew to come over to Grandma Ann's to find me. My friends lived in the neighborhood and I didn't have to be sitting in the house all day. I would leave the house around 2 p.m. and my grandparents wanted me back home before the streetlights cut on.

***

June was here and I was back with my mom. It was so boring over there, just dry, and quiet. Nobody really said anything to each other, just a daily flow going. I was talking on the phone a lot. I start talking to new people I met on social media. I knew better than to talk to strangers, but these were people that were my age. I didn't think there was anything wrong with that. I had two cellphones. I still had the phone my mom gotten me, but the service was off, and it was a trac phone. The one my mom got me, it still had all my numbers in it and the trac phone was for emergency reasons. I didn't use it because you had to buy the minutes you talked.

Mistreated, But Loved

One night I stayed on the phone past 1 a.m. She woke up and heard me on the phone.

She said, "RAH you better get your tail off this phone now. It's 1 o'clock in the morning and who you talking to?"

I hung up the phone so fast. Kim was a girl I met on Myspace. She was from Little Rock, Arkansas. We were the same age, and we were just having a good time talking. We talked about stuff like what her family was doing or mine, what she wanted to be when she grew up or me, we even talked about our moms. Her mom was on drugs so that's why she had so much freedom. Nobody was giving her a curfew. She could've been lying but it made me comfortable talking to her. We never got to meet in person though.

My mom never got this mad at me for being on the phone. She put me on punishment and told me I couldn't talk on the phone because I was misusing my privileges.

I said, "Ma please don't put me on punishment."

She said, "Get out my face before I make it longer than what it's gone be."

I cried to my room, closed the door, and beat up the pillows. I was so mad she did that. She could've given me another chance but *noooo*, she wanted to have that power like Randy. That controlling, 'you do what I say do or I'll make your life a living hell' power.

I kept saying to myself, "I can't wait to leave this fucking house forever. She was not acting like this when we were living on our own."

Maybe Randy was telling her how to treat me? I know that sounds crazy, but he would really do some low-down shit like that. She was becoming just like her husband. Then that day at Dr Frances office start playing in my head when I said we could

Mistreated, But Loved

come back to this place. He wanted us back so he could have my mom. He didn't even care about her; he just want control over her. I had to deal with it now.

I went over Grandma Lee's house to stay. She wasn't strict but she meant everything she said. Grandma Lee knew my mom didn't want me on the phone.

She told me, "Don't be on the phone, you know your mom told you not to be on it."

I was still sneaking on the phone. I thought she didn't know; I mean she wasn't saying anything. One night I must have stayed on for too long because she had come up the stairs and yelled at me for not listening. I was enjoying the freedom, I guess. Grandma Lee had to have told her that I was still talking, because how else could she have found out? I shouldn't have talked that long that night, but she didn't have to tell her.

My mom came and picked me up and I thought everything was cool. Kailey, my mom, and I were riding down the street acting as if nothing happened.

I thought everything would work out okay, until my mom said, "When we get home, you can give me that cell phone you got."

My stomach sunk down to my butt and Kailey just stared at me in awe. I wasn't even using the cellphone. I'm guessing Grandma Lee saw it while I was sleep or something.

I said to my mom, "I don't have a cell phone anymore, I threw it away."

She said, "You ain't threw away no phone. You think I'm crazy? I ain't gone say it no more."

I was not myself at all. I didn't care what happened to me, I just wanted to get away from her. Her attitude was becoming just like her husband. My mind was very irrational. I opened the door and tried to jump out. She grabbed me by my hair tightly and said with her teeth clinched together, "Get your tail back in here."

I closed the door. She let my hair go and we pulled off. Not even ten seconds later, I looked at her from my peripheral to make sure she wasn't paying attention. She was going 45 mph. I unlocked the door and jump out as fast as I could. I tumbled out so hard, I felt like I fell off a bike. My mom hit the brakes so hard and screamed because she didn't know what happened. The missing skin feeling from scrubbing the concrete was burning me. I had huge bloody scars on my back and shoulder. My shoe had come off and my shirt was ripped and bloody. I got up, found my shoe, and started walking down the street.

    I heard my mom asking the people driving by, "Did you see her jump out the car?"

No one responded, instead they just continued to drive on, looking concerned from their windows. My mom was trailing me, telling me to get in the car. I ignored her and kept walking. I just wanted her to let me be. Let me be free away from her. She called Randy and he came fast on his motor scooter from work. We were on Ross road by World Overcomers. When I saw him coming, I started running. He caught up to me and grabbed me by my shirt. He threw me against my mom truck like a bag of rocks and jacked me up like a dude that owed him money. I saw this man in his car coming out of his driveway. He was looking at the whole thing. He was biting his lip, as if he wanted to do something about it. It wasn't his business though. Randy opened my mom's truck door and threw me in. He didn't care how bloody or scarred up I was.

We were five minutes from my house, but my mom had made a quick stop. Randy trailed us the entire way, even as we stopped

Mistreated, But Loved

at the gate to drop off Kailey at my Aunt Dora's. My mom stopped right before the gate and called my Aunt to grab Kailey, so she didn't have to witness my punishment.

I begged, "Auntie, please take me with you!"

All she did was stare at me and then took my little sister back to her house.

My mom yelled, "You better shut up!"

I just sat there and cried with my hands folded in anger as my mom pulled off towards home. Before she even pulled up the driveway, I jumped out the truck and struck out running again. This time one of my cell phones fell. They were both in my bra. The one with my numbers fell out. I was trying to hide them, but Randy caught me. He had me on the ground punching me in the head and then dragged me in the house by my shirt. I tried to fight back this time, but I wasn't strong enough. My mom just sat there and watched him mistreat me, even when I knew she could have done something.

Once he was satisfied with whoopin' me, I escaped to my room and locked the door.

My mom then came to the door and said," I thought you threw the phone away. You just a liar."

Of course, I was lying to them. I had my other phone on me, and they didn't even know it. I was breathing hard and not to mention I was sore and bleeding from the scars. I just sat there and cried and cried and cried.

I called my dad in tears, barely breathing. I told him Randy just jacked me up and hit me.

He said in a very fast voice, "I'm on my way."

My dad came and he had the police with him. My mom and dad were outside talking to the police. I couldn't hear what they were talking about, but I was hoping my dad was going to do something. I opened my door, peaked out, looked left and right, then walked to the porch.

I said in a crying, frightened voice, "Daddy, please help me."

I didn't pay close attention because Randy came up behind me very fast. He grabbed me by the shoulders of my shirt from the back and dragged me back into the house. All I could do was scream and cry. I was still scarred up from the truck situation. My scars were still burning and bleeding. My dad was so angry and hurt because he couldn't protect me at the time. It wasn't his house, and they were married now. It was sort of like he had permission to discipline me now.

The police were just standing there. They didn't do anything either. They never did anything to help, ever. I couldn't hug my dad or anything. I cried myself to sleep that night. I was full of anger. I really wanted to wait until Randy and mom fell asleep to run away but I figured the police would be against me. They looked at me as if I were disobedient. I plotted and plotted on what I should've done but I was too scared to make any moves.

The next day I woke up and took a bath. My scars were burning as the water touched my skin. It felt like a dream the next day. I couldn't believe myself. My mom had the nerve to come and patch me up with band aids and Neosporin. I was still on punishment of course. I couldn't watch tv, get on the computer, talk on the phone, or go anywhere. I was in a room listening to my radio.

A couple days after that, my mom came in my room and said, "You not going back over your daddy or Grandma J's house until I feel I want you to, and you will be playing drums for Testament Chapel. You don't need to be around them because they let you do what you want. I'm your mother and you will respect me and this family."

I was confused, angry, and speechless. Tears just start rolling down my face and my heart felt like it was about to burst. She sounded just like Randy when she spoke. She was trying to push out my daddy and Grandma J in my life. He had to have gotten in her head about the whole thing. First off, they didn't let me do what I wanted, and I did respect the both of them. Before I knew it, the words, "I HATE YOU," were coming out of my mouth.

How could she remove me from the people that raised me and wanted nothing but the very best for me? That's my grandma and daddy that I love so much. She was hurting everybody. She even tried to hurt me by taking me from my home church. I had been a musician at Vernon Chapel since the age of five. Vernon Chapel was the church my dad was raised in, it is where I started playing drums at a young age. That's a natural gift that God gave me. That's all I knew, drums. I couldn't believe my mom just removed me from my church family like that, not to mention she stopped me from playing the drums there too. It was all very depressing. I didn't spend any time with my dad, Grandma J, or that side of the family; and that wasn't normal at all. I was heartbroken, so I can only imagine how my dad and Grandma J were feeling.

My mom said to me, "You can hate me all you want, but you gonna do exactly what I say and can't nobody do nothing about it, because I'm your mother."

I was so red in the face, crying my soul out. I couldn't call my dad or Grandma J because she took all the cordless phones in her room. I felt like I was in jail over there. I was so depressed, I had nothing to do. I didn't feel like anything or anybody because she made me feel totally hopeless. I loved my mom's side of the

Mistreated, But Loved

family, but I loved my dad's side of the family too and that's where I really wanted to be. I was being mistreated by my mom and it didn't make me feel any better. My mom was being irrational as hell with this decision. I just cried myself to sleep. It wasn't like I could do anything else. All I had was my radio. I remember listening to "Free" by Deniece Williams on V101.1 FM radio as I drifted off to sleep. I wanted to be free just like her.

***

That upcoming Sunday I went to Testament Chapel. Testament Chapel was Grandma Ann's home church. Instead of going to church and spending time with my dad and Grandma J, I was either at Grandma Ann's, Grandma Lee's, or Aunt Leo's house. Aunt Leo lived in Rossville, TN. Rossville, TN is the country. It's nothing but a lot of land, miles to get to your neighbor's house and it took forty minutes to get to the city. She was supposed to discipline me and change my attitude accordingly to how my mom said I was acting. Aunt Leo was one of Grandma Ann's older sisters. She was the one that everybody went to for everything. She was the cook, discipliner, and godmother of the family. I wasn't a disobedient child, I just had rebellious actions from the situations I was in.

When I got to church, I waited until the pastor preached and walked out the service to find a phone. I saw the church phone in the coat lobby. I picked up that phone and called my dad's cell phone so fast. I was shaking my leg, looking over my shoulder, trying to hide from anybody. I didn't want them telling anyone.

I kept saying, "Pick up, pick up, pick up, dad pleeeeease."

He picked that phone up and said, "Hello."

Mistreated, But Loved

I said really fast, "Hey dad, my mom said I can't see y'all no more. Please don't let her do that."

Next thing you know I burst out in tears on the phone with him. I felt the pain all over again from when my mom said it the first time.

He said, "It's ok baby, she can't do this. We gone fix it. Call me when you can, and I love you."

I said, "Okay dad, I love you too."

I wiped my face and walked back in church like nothing happened.

Grandma Ann let me see my dad once, but it was pointless. I was with Aunt Leo most of my summer. She stayed on the family land that my great-great grandfather left behind. It was a lot of land with three houses on it: Aunt Leo, Aunt Lavender and Aunt Barbra's house. My cousin Sheka lived next door to Aunt Leo. Aunt Lavender was Sheka's mother.

Sheka was four years older than me but we were close. We grew up together, so we knew each other very well. Us being together helped me be more comfortable but it was still not 'peaches and cream'. I was alone most of the day because Sheka had cheerleading practice and hung out with her friends. Of course, they were older and the opposite from me. I wasn't girly or glossy. I was tomboyish and nonchalant about how I carried myself. I went out with Sheka a few times but most of the time I was too young to go.

Sheka felt bad for me, especially the not being able to see my dad part. I said something about it to her every day because it bothered me. I was a hurt ass kid. I told her about that time Grandma Ann told me that I could see my dad for a quick second at the back gate, but I couldn't even touch him. I was confused on her statement.

Sheka said, "What? Now wait a minute! You couldn't touch your own daddy?"

I said, "I swear to you Sheka."

We just sat there, and she just tried to say things to make me feel better. The only thing that could've made me feel better was being back in my folks presence.

After hearing that, Sheka decided to take me to go see my dad. When we pulled up, I jumped out the car before the brakes were stopped all the way. I was overly excited to see my dad. I ran to him so fast and jumped on him. He picked me up and squeezed me so tight.

He said, "Daddy missed his baby so much!"

He was kissing me all over my face.

I said, "I missed you too dad!"

I'd never went that long without seeing him before and I know he missed my face. I could tell he missed me because he was squeezing the life out of me and he didn't want to let me go. He told me that the situation wasn't going to last forever. He said he got a lawyer, and he was taking my mom to court. I was ready for court to happen the next day, but we had a lot of time to go.

Dad said, "I'm demanding my rights as a father. She should not be keeping us from each other. This is wrong, she really pissed me off with this shit. Keeping my daughter from me like I ain't no good but that's ok. God don't like ugly and this right here what she doing, will never prosper. She won't win in the end baby, I promise you that. I'm in the middle of getting me a lawyer because we going to court."

My insides started having butterflies after he said all of that, but I kept it cool.

I said, "Yea dad, I just can't wait to be back with y'all."

Mistreated, But Loved

When he said *court*, all I could think about was him having full custody of me, Randy and my mom in jail and a whole lot of revenge in my favor. I know that sounded mean, but they treated me like I was nothing in my eyes. It wasn't that simple though. Trusting the process was the hardest part for me. I just didn't want to leave my dad and go back to the reality of not being able to be with him. My dad and I just kept hugging like we never wanted to let each other go. I didn't want to let go.

I kept saying in a trembling voice "I don't want us to depart dad."

He looked at me and said, "I know boo boo, me either, Daddy love his baby so much and can't nothing tear us apart not even this."

I started crying and he grabbed me and hugged me again.

He said, "Don't cry baby, it's gone be ok. I promise."

My dad thanked Sheka for bringing me to see him and we drove away. That feeling when I drove away was so painful. I felt my heart was in my throat. I couldn't believe I was in a situation like this. Not being able to see my dad or folks on that side was unbelievable because I was always there. Even though dad said we were going to court, I still had to deal with reality of being in this mess and that's what hurt so much.

12.

It was about to be my 10th grade year. It had been almost four months since I've spent time with my dad. I wished I were still going to my therapy appointments, because I needed to rant about all this stupidity that was going on. Somebody needed to talk some sense into my mom for real. My birthday was coming up and it was so depressing. I was still going to Rossville with Aunt Leo on weekends because I played drums on Sunday. I got to tell my friends face to face what was going on and boy, were they concerned. I just told them my dad was working on it and I'll be good soon.

I was still on punishment, but I did get to watch tv. Can you say, "Booooooooring!" I was happy to be leaving on Friday's and going over Aunt Leo's house. Sheka had said she was going to the movies in Collierville Saturday, and I told her I wanted to go too. She was going on a double date with her friend. I told her my friends were going to meet me at the movies and she could do her thing and I could do mine.

At this time of my life, I was sneaky, and I just wanted to have some fun and freedom. I was taken away from my family, my home church and then I couldn't even talk on the phone, watch TV or go anywhere. I just wanted to be free; free to have fun and live my life as the teenager I was.

I was about to be fifteen years old. I thought I was smart. She really was *iffy* about me going out with her, but she said okay. Saturday night had come, and I told my friends my plans. They said they didn't have a ride. I didn't care about that, I was not about to stay in the house, bored. I didn't tell Sheka nothing,

I just played it cool. Sheka had two sets of keys to her car. I took the other set and put them in my pocket. When we got to the movies, I told her to leave her phone with me because I needed to be able to call my friends. When her and her date went in the movies, I waited ten minutes to make sure everything was clear. I pulled off from the Collierville movie theater and went straight to East Memphis. East Memphis was only fifteen to twenty minutes from Collierville. I took the street way. I drove up Holmes Rd. all the way to Hacks Cross.

I picked up my homie Fabian and we pulled up on like two or three people in his neighborhood. They stayed close to Holmes Rd. I'm not even thinking about what time the movie would be over. Sheka's phone rang. I picked it up and it was her. She was so pissed off.

  I said to her, "Calm down, I'm down the street. I'll be there in a minute."

She started going off on me. She was talking too loud and so fast that I couldn't understand what she was saying, but she sounded super pissed. I hung the phone up on her to hurry myself up. I was twenty-five minutes away from the movies and I still had to drop Fabian off first. So, that made me five more minutes behind.

Let me inform you that, I didn't even have a permit. This was my first time being behind the wheel of a car by myself. For it to be my first time, I think I did good getting back fast and safe. I know that wasn't the point.

When I pulled up, she was standing there mad as hell.

  She said, "Get the hell out my seat. What the hell wrong with you? Where did you go?"

I just got out the car quickly and got in the back seat. I had to hear her talk all the way home. I regretted even doing anything

Mistreated, But Loved

just by hearing her talk. I knew she would be mad, but I didn't know she would feel this bad.

We pulled up to Aunt Leo house and she got out and ran to her house. I already knew I was about to be in trouble. I was coming off punishment a little bit but after this, back to jail I went. When my mom came and picked me up, I was so scared. I was wrong and I wish I would've thought better on it.

My mom said to me, "You are being a rebellious child and the Lord is shortening your days."

I know she wasn't talking about somebody being rebellious when she was just as rebellious as me. I wanted her and Randy to suffer so bad. I was happy anywhere but when I was in their presence. I knew I brought more punishment on myself after the situation. My spirit was becoming just like theirs. I was doing all kind of crazy stuff. They didn't trust me, and I didn't trust them. This was more reason they should've let me be where my love was reciprocated.

Grandma J and dad were trying to find a good lawyer. It took them some time, but Grandma J is so powerful in manifesting, she got connected with this attorney through a mutual friend. Grandma J's friend Ms. Margret told her about this attorney that she previously was going use to get a divorce. The attorney's name was Helen Jones. Mrs. Jones was one of the best family law attorneys in Memphis.

They had got the best lawyer on this side of the earth. They gave her all the information she needed for the case. Just let me say the process was slower than a turtle racing a cheetah. I never got to sit in court with them. I was hoping every time it was over, they would say I could be with my dad.

What I did find out was that my mom was breaking some laws. When her and my dad divorced, I was supposed to be going over his house on weekends anyway. They had made

Mistreated, But Loved

an agreement back when they first got divorced, but my mother was not holding up to her end. Everything was going so well all those years with sharing me but then *boom*, she completely took me out of their lives. She couldn't have thought this was right. Anybody with common sense would know this was uncalled for and just wrong. I wonder did Grandma Ann and papa tell her this was wrong? They should've told her if they didn't.

Everybody was always used to me being with Grandma J and when they noticed I wasn't around, questions where being asked. People were all kinds of concerned and nosey. My dad and I were so supported, I remember the pastor and minister of music being there for us at court. All this was going on and I just wanted one answer from the judge. I just didn't want another Christmas to go by without me spending it with my dad and that side of the family.

    They finally went back to court and this time the judge gave my mom simple orders. I was to go over my dad house every other weekend starting at 6 pm on Friday and come back at 6 pm on Sunday. It was short but at least I got to spend time with my people. I couldn't wait until that Friday came. I talked about it all week to my friends, really to everybody.

When my daddy pulled up, I was literally running to get into the car. When I got in the car, he hugged me so tight. We were so excited, both of us were smiling from ear to ear. It felt so good to be back to normal in my daddy's presence. I couldn't wait to pull up to Grandma J's house because I couldn't wait to see her, nana, and Uncle Castro. Dad kept saying how much everybody missed me and they couldn't wait to see me. I ran in the house, they were just as happy as I was. Nana and Uncle Castro had cooked and of course I ate all that I wanted. I slept so well that night. Everything felt just right.

I stopped going to Aunt Leo's house on weekends to play drums at Testament Chapel. My position as a musician had continued at Vernon Chapel. I played drums every other Sunday. I was back with my church family and everything was feeling good. At 6pm on Sunday I was so sad because I was pulling back up at Randy house. When I walked backed in that house, my spirit changed to something bitter.

13.

My mom started going to church more. It was time for a spiritual change. She would always take Kailey and I with her. It seemed liked my mom was trying to help Randy too, but he needed some type of special help for his attitude. I think the demons had him locked up in hell with no key to release him.

On the weekends I wasn't going over my dad's house, I was still going to church on Sundays. My mom started taking us to World Overcomers and all of us got involved in something. We even went to bible study on Wednesday. The youth had their own ministry, so that's where I was. Being involved with others my age was really fun, I hated to leave most of the time. I played drums for the youth sometimes and I was always going to the lock-ins and fun activities they had. I loved going to church.

Some of my classmates even went there, so it was another place to enjoy myself away from the house. It wasn't taking away from Vernon Chapel, so I was happy. I was just an all-around person.

School was going well. I wasn't getting on punishment anymore and I was getting more involved with friends and J.R.O.T.C. That was another get away for me. We had practice after school, but we also got to treat our classroom like a home.

Major Buck always treated us like his own. If they weren't involved in activities in J.R.O.T.C, they didn't know Major Buck personally. I can say he did come off as an asshole to other kids, but they were more than likely disrespectful anyway.

Major Buck told us right from wrong and wanted nothing but the best for his students.

***

In July 2009, Grandma Lee ended up getting sick and she had to go to the hospital. I remember a couple years back when she slipped and fell backwards on the floor at the restaurant. She hit her head hard. Everybody that saw her, ran to her quickly. They helped her off the floor. She didn't go see a doctor or anything. I thought that she should, but older folks like to doctor on themselves. Since the doctors said they didn't know what was wrong with her, I guessed it could've been from that. I went to go see her and when I walked in her room, she was not looking like herself. She was barely sitting up and her tongue was sticking out a little. It hurt my feelings to see her in that position. My mom, Aunt Amelia, and some others were praying and speaking life into her. I loved her just like she was my own grandma. Her sons were so hurt, they just had given up hope because of how things looked.

Her sisters and brothers kept saying, "God has the last say."

We went home that night in silence. My mom woke me up the next morning and told me Grandma Lee had passed.

I just cried loud, "Noooo!"

Grandma Lee was the glue that kept the family together. So now that she was gone, I wondered how things were about to be now? The funeral went well. Everything happened so fast. Everybody was still getting together and having family dinner. The tradition was still happening, but it felt funny because Grandma Lee was now gone. There was an empty spot in everybody's heart.

Mistreated, But Loved

At this point, Randy and I weren't really saying anything to each other anymore. I didn't care if he liked me or not. He didn't have to treat me like his own. I was completely over him, his attitude and everything else when Grandma Lee passed.

I was fifteen years old now. I had been dealing with bullshit since this man came into my life. I was even over my mom because she was so caught up into him, she was blind from all the things she was supposed to been paying attention to, like me. I know she was going to church, but she still wasn't herself. She could've gotten better quicker if she only just left Mr. Evil alone. He was so toxic; his spirit could drain anybody and make them feel like nothing.

Between July and December 2009, Randy was turning into an alcoholic and his attitude was beyond everybody's. Grandma Lee was not here anymore. I know that had to hurt him from a deep place. His toxic traits were just getting worse than they were when she was here on earth.

Christmas was around the corner, but I could tell my mom was not really too fond of him. She was trying to build her a better relationship with God and Randy was not aligning with anything. He should've been by himself. If it wasn't about him then he didn't care.

I hoped to be with Grandma J and dad for the entire Christmas. I always wanted to spend the whole Christmas with them. I would usually go see them for a little while and go to Randy's folk's house. I figured since Grandma Lee had passed, we weren't going to do anything. She was the cook and the loving one. She used to call everybody on holiday mornings to tell us what time dinner was. However, I only went to spend a little time with my dad to get my gifts from his side of the family. We still ended up going to Grandma Lee and Grandpa's house most of the day, but nothing was the same. It wasn't that many people over and the

Mistreated, But Loved

food tasted different. I was used to us having a great time with dancing, laughter and just fun. Not this Christmas though. The new year was here, and the big change was coming.

Randy had lost his mind all together. I was going over my dad's house on weekends. There was a lot I didn't see that Kailey did. Kailey and Randy were inseparable. She just loved her dad so much. One night my mom and Randy had gotten into a heated argument while Kailey was there. He pushed Kailey out the room and locked the door. She was screaming because she said Randy was hitting my mom in the bedroom. She could hear my mom screaming and saying Stop! Kailey was a smart little girl, she called Grandma Ann and papa to come over. She said her dad was hitting my mom. They came over quickly and got them. My mom packed all our clothes and went to Grandma Ann and papa's house. Kailey was so scared. She finally saw how crazy her dad was.

It was Fall break, so I stayed a few more days with my dad. I didn't know what was going on, I was just happy to be with my dad. When it was time to go back with my mom, I went over Aunt Dora's house. My mom told me we were going to be staying over there for a while until we get our own place. Our own place? Was she leaving Randy again? They were married. I thought she loved him. I can't lie, she was acting different with him. She wasn't even taking Kailey over his house anymore. This was deeper than it had ever been.

My mom said this was the last straw and that she couldn't take it anymore. I found out Randy didn't know where we were. My mom was hiding from him. Aunt Amelia, his own sister helped us get away from him. I heard him on the speaker phone telling Aunt Amelia he didn't know what was wrong. He was trying to say all the right things for us to come back but my mom didn't say a word. She didn't want to talk to or see Randy. Was she serious about leaving this time? They just got married the year before. I knew it was a bad idea to go back. I was hoping she was serious for real. We were so peaceful without him the last time.

We moved with Aunt Dora for a month or less. I could tell we were getting in her way. I'd have to say it was a small space over there for all four of us. She stayed in a one-bedroom apartment with one bathroom. We eventually moved into our own apartment. I had my own space, but Kailey always wanted to be in the room with me. Of course, as a big sister I told her to get out when I was on the phone. I didn't want her snitching and telling my mom about my conversations on the phone. It didn't matter if we struggled or not, I would rather had struggled than to be in Randy's presence.

My mom said we were not going back no matter what. For some reason I believed her this time. He was calling my mom phone every day, leaving crazy voicemails and text messages. I listened to one and he told my mom she had a Jezebel spirit. As psychotic as he was, he had the nerve to call her Jezebel. He was demonic all together. God needed to come down to earth personally and straighten him up because nobody here on earth seemed to teach him a lesson.

14.

Months went by and he still called and harassed my mom. Randy didn't know where we lived though. I wouldn't be surprised if he did though. That fool was crazy. It wasn't no telling what he would have done to my mom or us. Kailey didn't even want to be around him. This fool's only child was scared of him. How could a parent continue to be foolish when they are supposed to set examples for their seeds?

We lived our lives peacefully again. It was peaceful as long as he wasn't around. The only person that was there for us from Randy's family was Aunt Amelia. If we needed anything, she would always help. She had a spirit just like Grandma Lee. If only she could talk sense into her brother like Grandma Lee did. We were going to church more and more. I start to see a change in my mom. She was really trying to be the best she could be. When she stopped smoking cigarettes, I knew she was trying to reach her full potential.

My mom started dating this gospel rapper and minister. Elijah Howard was his name. Elijah grew up with my mom at her childhood church. His family and my family all knew each other. Elijah was a nice man. He was a God-fearing man and a good father in my eyes. Kailey and Elijah Jr. played sometimes, and they got along with each other greatly. I could see Elijah Jr. being my little brother. I always wanted a little brother anyway.

My mom or dad weren't having any more kids. This would've been good for all of us. We even had a dinner one time just for Elijah and my mom's family. I liked how everything was going, especially for my mom. She was happy with Elijah. She just wanted to have a family and be a wife. I played drums and

Elijah was a gospel rapper. I had never heard of a gospel rapper before. After I heard his first song "Doing it for Jehovah" I was intrigued. He rapped about living his life for Christ. The first rap song I heard with no cursing. This was a positive act.

I was ready to go to shows and maybe sometimes perform too. I finally liked somebody my mom was dating. Even though her and Randy were separated, I knew she wasn't going back to him. I figured divorcing him had to be coming soon.

When we got on our own, my mom stopped tripping about my dad and Grandma J. She let me go over there every weekend and didn't have a problem if I wanted to stay a little longer. All that court stuff and now this. We didn't even have to go through that miserable shit. I guess experience is the best teacher. I wasn't on lock down or unhappy anymore.

My friends and I were doing a lot of stuff. Trouble was something we didn't get into. I was hanging out with them more outside of the neighborhood. I had friends with cars, so we were all over the city doing teenager stuff. I had more freedom to do what I wanted to do. Every day when I woke up, I hoped that my friends and I would catch Randy slipping around my crib. Me and my friends were going to beat him up. My friends knew what was going on and they were ready for the hype. They had never met Randy before and hated him for the things I had told them.

Benzy and Truly were different though. They were my big homies. I called them my big homies because they were older than me, always had my back, supported me, and made sure I was good. I started hanging out with them a lot when my mom left Randy. It was always the three of us. My folks thought I was down the street, but I was all in orange mound or around town with Benzy and Truly. I thought this was the best time of my life. I was enjoying it so much because I was doing new things

Mistreated, But Loved

and getting more attention. I was 16 and smelling myself as grown folk would say.

It was my 11th grade year, and the summer was almost here. They always say when something is going well, something is always there to change the day. I found out my Uncle Castro was sick. He had lung and liver cancer. This was the worst for my family. This was my favorite uncle we are talking about. I watched him get sicker and sicker. That hurt me to see him like that. Uncle Castro was a strong man. Grandma J, Nana, my dad and his kids took good care of him. I was one of his kids too, that was always known. He fought that sickness for a long while. I used to help watch him sometimes on weekends when Grandma J and them would be gone. I was just happy to be able to spend time with him. He still put a little beer in his food sometimes. That was a secret he didn't want nobody to know.

One day while I was over Grandma J's house, Benzy and Truly pulled up on me.

We were outside chilling in the car, and I asked Truly, "What's that smell?"

She said, "What this? This weed rolled up. I'm smoking a blunt."

In my mind I'm like, "So this what everybody be smoking?"

I wanted to hit it and feel what all my friends had been feeling. When I smoked it, I didn't feel anything. Was I doing it right?

I told Truly, "I'm not high at all. I feel the same way."

She said, "Just swallow it, cover your mouth, and blow it out of your nose."

I did that about two or three times. I was on a cloud so high, I kept laughing and wiping my face. I got so hungry; I ordered a

Mistreated, But Loved

pizza right there in the car. When the pizza got there, I attacked it quickly.

Truly said, "Calm down youngin, you supposed to enjoy the high. You about to eat it away."

I said, "I need to eat some of it down, I'm too up there." It was just a hilarious moment.

The weed had me in slow motion and ready to go to sleep. I think I had a bit much. I went straight to sleep when I went back in the house. I got caught by Nana one night. I enjoyed the feeling of being high. I was upstairs in my bathroom smoking with the window up.

Nana came to the steps and said, "I can't believe you. Up there smoking that stuff."

I said, "No mam, I'm not smoking anything." I tried keeping a straight face, but my voice continued to falter.

She said, "Yes you are, I can smell it," with a higher pitched voice than usual.

There was nothing else I could say. I was caught red handed and so nervous. I was disappointed that nana knew I did this, and I was really hoping she didn't tell Grandma J or my dad. I didn't know how they would feel, and I never wanted to disappoint them as well. They always said, "Say NO to drugs."

Days had gone by and nobody had said anything to me about it. Every time I saw Grandma J or my dad, my palms started sweating. I would say to myself, "Please don't bring it up. Please don't bring it up." They didn't say anything, and I didn't either. I wasn't smoking every day, just sometimes.

It was about to be summertime and my senior year was approaching. I didn't care about moving out so quick because we weren't with Randy anymore. I was feeling so free, I was becoming one person all the time. That spirit of not wanting to be somewhere, was over. I soon realized I was smiling every day.

I stopped seeing Elijah, even though he was around all the time. I asked my mom where he had been, and she said they had broken up. I didn't understand why because he was so nice and sweet to my mom. I thought he for sure liked her. Did this mean we were going back to Randy? I wasn't going, I didn't care what the plans were.

Elijah was just like the other men. I found out that it didn't matter if somebody was God fearing or not. A man is a man. All this time, he was engaged to another woman. How so? Nothing was really adding up to me. He was always hanging with us, but he was about to get married to a whole other person. I know my mom was hurt. Who wouldn't be? The luck my mom had with men were just not lining up. Maybe God was saying, 'Sit down and heal first.' And she needed to listen!

Even though she probably was super hurt, she didn't let me see it. My mom wasn't focusing on any man anymore. She was focused more on herself and her children.

After I started smoking weed, my feelings stopped caring about a lot. I didn't overthink anymore, just relaxed. My mom walked in the house one night while I was high. I was so nervous. I remember I was making a salad at the time. When she started speaking, I thought I was caught.

She said, "You know I'm sorry for making you suffer all these years. I really didn't protect you. I let this man come in and do all this stuff. I'm just so sorry for everything. I was lost, confused and out of my mind but I know better now."

The tears started rolling down her face and I felt bad because I saw the change she was trying to make and plus this was my mom.

80

Mistreated, But Loved

I said, "Ma it's okay. I love you and we not there no more."

I didn't care what had happen in the past, I forgave my mom just like that. I just wanted her to love me and be on my side. I don't know why my heart was so forgiving. Seems like we were always against each other when she was with Randy.

Mistreated, But Loved

15.

We had been living in the apartment for a while and everything was going well. My mom and I weren't arguing. Kailey and I even got better with loving each other. She looked up to me and always wanted to be around me. My mom was actually letting me be a young adult. I could go anywhere as long as I told her where I was going and who I was going with. I was gone all the time. I wasn't telling her everything all the time. What teenager actually does though?

Truly and Benzy were still coming to see me. They had me out all night sometimes my mom would get upset with me. I had to make up stuff like, the car got a flat or we ran out of gas. I was so young and stupid. My mom knew I was lying but she didn't do any extreme punishments. I didn't even get on punishment. She would just say I couldn't go out the next time, but she was just upset at the time.

The summer was here, and I felt even more free. In the daytime I was always trying to go somewhere or have company while my mom was at work. I had everybody over while she was at work. She would've killed me if she'd known I had people over there. Nobody ever stole or damaged anything. I was always picky about who I was friends with. I was a respectful person so everybody and everyone I hung around was respectful as well.

I ended up staying at Grandma J and Grandma Ann's house most of the summer. I was with Truly and Benzy almost every day. I used to tell my grandma's I was going down the street, but my big homies were waiting on me at the corner in the car.

82

Mistreated, But Loved

As long as I was at home by the time the sun went down, I was good. I was about to be a senior and I planned on turning up the whole year.

My first day of my senior year made me feel so good. I had to do something different this year. I wanted a job to make my own money. I wanted to buy clothes my mom didn't want to buy me. My mom was a member of World Overcomers church and they bought the Hickory Ridge Mall. They were putting an Incredible Pizza in the mall. They were hiring starting at the age 16. That was great because I was about to be 17. My mom helped me fill out the application and it felt like I was writing a paper. It was only long because my mom didn't have patience. This was my first time doing a job application. Her patience was really thin and short. I hated to ask her questions sometimes because I didn't want to disturb her nerves. I think all teenagers felt like me when they had parents with short patience.

It was August but the job started in October. They called me in September and told me I had gotten the job. I was about to be making my own money. I was still in J.R.O.T.C on the drill team and being active.

On Wednesday I was going over my homeboy Cliff house. Cliff and I were in J.R.OT.C together and he'd been my homeboy since 4th grade. He was the weirdest, coolest friend I had. We used to do stuff like drive his mom's truck on mud hills, repel out of trees with ropes, shoot each other with the pellet guns and all kinds of crazy stuff. I remember one time we shot a squirrel out the tree. Cliff skinned him and put him on the grill. That was my first-time eating squirrel, but it was actually pretty good. He stayed close to Randy's house. The more we rode by his house, the more I wanted revenge for all the things he put me through. I could not let go of the hatred I had for him. He was going to have to pay for this damage. I had friends in gangs. They had my back, and I knew they would handle dude

Mistreated, But Loved

for me. They asked me all the time, "You want us to take him out. He really doesn't get to bother you no mo." I could see it in their eyes they were ready to do damage, but I said, "Naw y'all, I don't want y'all in my drama. He gone get his."

October was finally here, and I was about to start working. It was a lot of us working there. Ages 17-60 was working at Incredible Pizza. I had fun every day at work. It was bigger and better than Chucky Cheese. I was a host and I bussed tables. I was a busy 17-year-old. On weekends I went over Grandma J house and worked until closing. On weekdays I was going to school, having J.R.O.T.C practice and went to work maybe twice on a school night. My friends and I still got to kick it during my free time.

Uncle Castro and Kailey had the same birthday.

If he had a party, he always said, "Make sure y'all get Kay a cake too."

He was the only person that called her that. He never wanted to leave her out. Even though uncle wasn't Kailey's blood uncle, he treated her just like his own. She loved uncle just as much. We had a huge party for him even though he was sick. He looked sick but he was so happy to see everyone there that he loved. We all had a great time, ate good and fellowship with each other. I never seen uncle cry until this day. He barely could talk but the smile on his face told you it all.

Remember I said when something is going well, something is always there to change the day. Uncle Castro passed away the month of November. My mom woke me up and told me the news. I was so crushed. I knew he was sick but for him to actually be gone. That was a hard pill to swallow. I didn't want to face the reality of it. This was the first person that passed away who I loved so deeply. I loved Grandma Lee, but uncle was different. He has been there since the day I was born. He was more than my uncle; he was more of a grandfather to me.

16.

January 2011 was finally here. The year I walked across that stage. My mom was doing her best with building a better relationship with me. I loved my mom; I just didn't know how to be myself completely around her. She had to get to know me. Even though I was her child, she didn't know me personally. I was just glad I didn't have a hatred feeling towards her anymore. If it wasn't for her dating that fool, life probably could've been better for the both of us. Each experience further withered away our bond and relationship as a family. All I wanted, for all those years, was for my mom to love me and treat me like a priority; because she *wanted* to, not because she *had* to. So, it took time for me to let her in. When she talked to me, it felt like she was a stranger. A bond that was once nonexistent, had somehow come to be—it was broken and needed work.

My mom came to me and told me we were moving out of the apartment. I'm thinking like, "Where are we going?"

She said, "I'm going back to school to be a radiologist. I won't be able to work and go to school, so we're moving back home with momma and daddy. You will be living with Grandma J because you already got your own room and stuff over there."

I said with an exciting tone, "Okay. When are we moving?"

I was so excited; I could've moved that day. When I talked to Grandma J on the phone, she was so happy. My mom had already called her and asked could I stay. Of course, Grandma J

Mistreated, But Loved

said yes with no hesitation. We literally moved the next week. Quick enough for me.

Papa put my clothes and all the stuff I was keeping on the back of his truck. When we pulled up to drop my stuff off, I could almost burst in tears. All I could think about was all these years of bullshit, hate and chaos I went through. This is the exact place my mom and Randy were keeping me away from. Now she needed me to be there.

It's funny how God work. It was all about what Randy wanted, now Randy is alone and I'm getting what I want. All the pain and suffering I went through and I still end up at the place I wanted to be. I planned on moving out my last day of graduation, but God moves mountains we can't see. The school year went on and I finished my senior year happy and with a 4.0. Things were really different. I was going into adulthood and I was about to get ready for college. The relationship with my mom and I was getting better and better. As we got to know each other as people, we learned how to respect each other in healthier ways. I will always respect her as my mother but also as a person. The forgiving and upholding heart that I have, gives me the power of love.

Acknowledgements

First, I want to thank God for protecting me as I went through being a rebellious, abused, and neglected kid. As well as, lifting me up through those constant feelings of hopelessness. My faith allowed me to gain the strength and wisdom I needed to grow into be the person I am today.

I would also like to acknowledge Jeanett Ballentine, Rodderrick Hayes, Janie Mae Hughes, Kacey Plummer, Callie Farmer, the entire Mae Fam, Trudy Dudley, Tya Thomas, April Plummer, Memphis Shaw, Mario Brudley, Millionaire Grind Family, and my editors, Lillian Taylor & Emily Boykin for helping and inspiring me to write this book.

Made in the USA
Columbia, SC
26 November 2021